JONATHAN PINNOCK was born in Bedford, England and studied Mathematics at Cambridge University. He subsequently stumbled into a career in software development and has been there ever since. Somewhere along the way he wrote one book on software development and co-wrote a further twelve. His preference, however, is for fiction and his first novel *Mrs Darcy versus the Aliens* was published by Proxima in 2011. His short stories have won numerous prizes and have been widely published. He is married with two slightly grown-up children, several cats and a 1961 Ami Continental Jukebox. He blogs at www.jonathanpinnock.com.

Also by Jonathan Pinnock

Mrs Darcy versus the Aliens

JONATHAN PINNOCK

DOT DASH

SALT

CROMER

PUBLISHED BY SALT PUBLISHING
12 Norwich Road, Cromer NW1 3ER United Kingdom

© Jonathan Pinnock, 2012

Printed in the UK by TJ International Ltd, Padstow, Cornwall

Typeset in Paperback 9 / 10

ISBN   978 1 84471 882 5 paperback

1 3 5 7 9 8 6 4 2

To Gail, as always

CONTENTS

NOT SO MUCH A ROUGH GUIDE

The travel guide was accurate, if a tad unhelpful. "For more information about Hell," it said, "see below."

RZR AND NAPOLEON

rZr takes the photograph out of his pocket and looks at it one last time. He shakes his head and puts it away again. He adjusts his balaclava and re-positions his mask. He puts on a new pair of latex gloves and switches on the airbrush. Once he would have used standard industrial spray cans, but that was back in the day when he was daubing trains. rZr steps back and surveys the wall that is his canvas.

"Edgy," he says to himself. "I'll give you fucking edgy."

The room smells of polish and leather and one wall is taken up with a vast map of the world, covered in pins. There are half a dozen people sitting around the table apart from rZr. He and Miranda are the only ones not wearing suits: Miranda because she is the only woman present and rZr because he is rZr. They are heavily outnumbered but they are calling the shots.

"It really would be much easier to do this if Mr . . . rZr . . . would remove his balaclava," the prick from marketing is saying. Miranda glances at rZr. He shakes his head.

"rZr will remain anonymous for the duration of this commission," she says. "rZr's anonymity is concomitant with his role as a guerrilla artist and it would not be appropriate for him to break his normal mode of working, even for such an important client as yourselves."

"It's just that it's . . . a bit . . . odd having to deal with—"

"You deal with me, as rZr's representative," says Miranda, noticing rZr's scribbled note saying *CLOSE THE FUCKER DOWN NOW*. "rZr is only here to observe and ensure that he is happy with the way that the negotiations are handled." She pauses, making sure that she has the agreement of everyone in the room. No one objects. "So, if we could continue to point 14.3, creative control. This is particularly important for rZr as there are those who would construe that his integrity as an artist might be compromised by the very act of talking to people such as yourselves—"

"Well, he isn't exactly talking to us, is he—"

"—and it is therefore essential to the success of the project that rZr is allowed to have complete creative—"

"Absolutely," says the smoothie next to the prick from marketing. He was introduced as being responsible for corporate art procurement, although this is his first contribution to the meeting. "We have long had a policy here of investing in cutting-edge art and we specifically set out to hire rZr as part of this ongoing process. In fact, the mural for the chairman's office is one of the more significant acquisitions that we are likely to make this quarter."

The prick from marketing raises his eyebrows at this, but the chairman shakes his head. rZr looks hard at him. He knows a surprising amount about the chairman, and very little of it tallies with the charming, physically unassuming man sitting opposite him. When he walked into the room, he was five foot nothing. Small man, big ambition, thinks rZr. Like Napoleon. Now there's an idea.

"I'm with Peter on this," says the chairman, gesturing at the procurement guy. "We do this properly. If it's got to be edgy, then edgy it is."

"But, surely, given the amount we're spending on this—" says the prick from marketing.

ANY MORE OF THIS AND IM OFF, writes rZr. *FUCK THIS SHIT.*

"If I can interject," says Miranda. "Maybe if I show you

some current selling prices for rZr's work, it might make this discussion irrelevant." She passes across a piece of paper and all five of them on the opposite side of the table study it with interest.

"We're in the wrong business," says the prick from marketing. No one laughs.

"So, if we can move on? The next point concerns the schedule for the transfer of funds into the numbered bank account—"

Usually, he has only the vaguest of ideas about what he's going to paint when he begins work on a wall. But this time, he's thought long and hard about it and he knows exactly what he's going to do. He starts in the middle and paints a large caricature of Napoleon with a bare arse and the chairman's face. Yeah. Nice. Then he starts to work outwards from there. After a while, rZr tightens the strap on his mask as the room begins to fill with solvent fumes.

Miranda and rZr are leaving the building by the underground car park, as specified in the contract. She pauses as they emerge from the liftwell.

"Well, I think we're due a celebration, aren't we?" she says.
"Not yet," says rZr.

"Jesus Christ, r, we've just screwed over one of the biggest, bastardest corporations in the world. Aren't you happy?"

"No. Not yet."

She looks at him. "I don't get you, r. Maybe it's because I can never see your face behind that stupid balaclava, but—"

"Let's just say I'm playing a long game here, and it's not over yet."

She scrutinises his face again. "I don't even understand why you're doing this. I don't get it. OK, I guess I understand why you've gone corporate. It happens to everyone eventually. But you still seem—"

"Conflicted? Yeah. Maybe I am. Listen, I'd love to stand

here talking to you, but I need to have a bath. Being in that place makes me feel dirty, y'know?"

"Sure . . . sure. Maybe we'll go for a drink . . . some other time?"

"Yeah, sure. Maybe. Whatever."

rZr watches Miranda leave and then heads off in the opposite direction into the backstreets. When he's sure that no one's looking, he takes off his balaclava and takes a deep breath. Not long now. He emerges into the sunlight and heads off towards the tube. The photograph is burning a hole in his pocket.

rZr is almost finished now. He's pleased with some of the details he's managed to insert in there, especially some of the hidden references to the corporation's covert activities in various mineral-rich African basket cases. rZr has done his research and he knows exactly what he is dealing with here.

The prick from marketing is studying the finished work, glass of wine in hand.

"It's very green, is it not?" he says.

"rZr is working a lot in green at the moment," says Miranda, improvising. rZr, standing aloof from the rest of the crowd, gives the slightest of nods.

"Well, I don't know a lot about art," says the prick from marketing. "Think most of it's a load of bollocks. But I suppose I can see something in it. Not terribly edgy, though, is it, apart from the strange froggy geezer mooning in the middle of it all?"

"rZr says that there are hidden layers in there."

"Oh, I see. Subtlety. You surprise me. I thought you arty types just liked painting dog turds and stuff like that. Still, Sir Michael seems to like it, so that's all that matters." He gestures to a waiter. "Top up, please!"

"Do you ever take the balaclava off?" says Peter from corporate art, sidling over.

"No, he doesn't," says Miranda. "Well, I've never seen him without it."

"Really? How extraordinary. I thought you two were—"

Miranda smiles. "Er . . . no . . . I mean—"

Peter raises an eyebrow and walks away.

"Sorry about that," says Miranda.

rZr leans close to her and whispers, "I've had enough of this shit. Let's go."

She gives him an odd look, and then says, "OK." She puts down her drink and follows him out of the room. The rest of the party are watching as Sir Michael discusses various aspects of his new mural with several hangers-on. rZr wonders how soon it will be before the chairman gets the hidden message.

They pause briefly in the corridor outside the chairman's office. It's almost as if Miranda's waiting for him to do something. And Christ knows, he'd like to do it with her, right in that room opposite, right on the fucking boardroom table. But this has never been about pleasure. He shakes his head. He takes the crumpled photograph out of his pocket and hands it to her. She looks at it and stares back at him.

"I've got to go," says rZr.

The work on the new clinic is going well – and not a moment too soon, as the facilities in the villages nearby can no longer cope with this onslaught of chronic illness. You could be forgiven for wondering which god is taking his vengeance on them, and what they have done to offend him. But even these people, whom circumstance has denied anything other than the most basic of education, know exactly what has caused it.

rZr is almost happy for the first time in years. Provided that the trucks can get through with a few more loads before the rains start, phase one of the project should be completed on schedule. They'll have to wait a few months before they can start on the orphanage, but in Africa you have to work with nature, not against it. And then he has to organise the recruitment of the staff, so he'll need to double-check how many of them the interest on that Swiss account is going to pay for.

His second mobile rings and as ever it amuses him that in Africa you can be eight hours' journey down a dirt track and still pick up a perfect signal. He enjoys ironies like that. The call will have been routed through untraceable forwarding accounts in at least eight other countries to get to him. He recognises the number. He's been waiting for this call.

"Miranda, hi," he says.

"Er, hi." She sounds nervous. It's the first time they've spoken for several months.

"So what can I do for you?"

"Christ, you sound a long way away."

"Maybe, but I bet the weather's nicer here."

"Listen, r, you know that photograph you gave me?"

"Yeah?"

"The kid in it . . . the poor thing . . . was it . . . arsenic?"

"Yeah."

"Shit." There's a long silence. rZr waits.

"There's something I need to tell you," says Miranda. The tone in her voice has shifted slightly, and rZr's heart skips a beat.

"Yeah?"

"Something odd's happened. Remember Sir Michael whatsit? The chairman?"

rZr can barely breathe. "Yeah?"

"He's . . . he's . . . dead."

He can't help smiling, although his heart is now thumping away like a steamhammer. "Really? Well, I can't say I—"

"Shut up, r. He's been poisoned. I mean, can you imagine it? And with arsenic, too."

rZr says nothing.

"r, this isn't something you've done, is it? I mean, I don't know how, but—"

He pauses.

"r?"

He takes a deep breath. "Did you ever hear the story about how Napoleon died?"

"Sorry?"

"They say he was killed by toxins leaking from his wall-paper. Arsenic compounds." He looks over towards the new clinic. "That shit can fuck you up in all sorts of ways, you know. Ask anyone living near the run-off from a mine."

"You're scaring me, r."

"But you don't get arsenic in wallpaper any more, do you? Or in paint. Usually. But if you want an extra-specially vivid green, what you really need is Emerald Green." He pauses. "Also known as copper acetoarsenite."

"Oh my God, but that mural—"

He doesn't say anything.

"r?"

"Look, it's probably best we don't talk for much longer. Been good working with you, but I've got things to do."

"r—"

"As of this moment, I'm not called rZr any more, Miranda. I'm just another nameless guy in Africa. Forget everything you ever knew about me." With that, he switches the phone off, removes the SIM card and crushes it under his foot. Closure.

And then, walking towards him, emaciated and unsteady on her feet, is the woman in the photograph. Limping next to her is the child that she was carrying in it. His feet are mis-shapen and turn in on themselves. The woman holds out an unsteady hand to the artist formerly known as rZr.

"Thank you," she says, bowing.

He shakes his head. He doesn't want her gratitude. He doesn't want anyone's gratitude. It's personal, this, and it always has been. He gives a half smile and turns away from her, in time to see a group of men struggling to unload an operating table from the lorry. "Hey!" he shouts, "You take care with that thing."

THE DROUGHT

When she met him, the rain stopped, the clouds parted and the sun shone once more. The drought lasted the rest of her life.

CONVALESCENCE

I hate it here. Two more weeks and I'll be safe to travel, but for now I'm stuck in the Sunshine Inn, sitting on the end of the bed, pushing buttons on the remote, trying to find a station that talks something like sense. The news. There's a war on somewhere. It's going badly. People are getting killed. An actress I've never heard of has filed for divorce. Someone bad has been executed. Well, they say he's bad. So that's OK, then. Six o'clock and all's well with America.

She came again last night. I must ask them about that tomorrow. I think she's asking me for something. Begging, even. The headaches have gone now, which is something. I just want to go home.

There are three people opposite me this time – my physician, the surgeon, and (this is new) a psychiatrist. Dr Newcombe is pleased with the results of my tests. My vision seems to be close to what it was two years ago, before all this started. I haven't had any more blackouts. My balance seems good, and my bloods are normal. One more check-up in a week's time, and I can be signed off. Well, that wasn't worth turning up for.

They are clearly expecting me to leave. The psych and the surgeon are already putting their papers away.

"Is there anything else you want to ask?" says Dr Newcombe.

"Well, yes," I begin, then I hesitate. It seems so silly. "It's just, I've been sort of seeing things."

"Seeing things?" All three are now looking at me. "You mean dreams?"

"No – well, yes, sometimes they are dreams. But sometimes they happen when I'm wide awake."

"Visions, then?"

"I suppose you could call them that. There's a young girl . . ."

Dr Newcombe and the psych exchange the briefest of glances.

"Could you describe her?" asks the psych.

An odd question. Strangely, though, I *can* describe her. I've seen her so many times in the last few weeks.

"She's around eleven to twelve years old. Blonde hair. Wearing a red party frock. I'm holding her by the hand and she's talking to me quite insistently. Begging me for something."

Raised eyebrows all round. It's Dr Newcombe who responds.

"Mr Sanderson, you have undergone radical surgery. It would be extremely unusual for you not to be experiencing some kind of mild psychological trauma. That's why we've asked my colleague Dr Berkowitz to join us." He nods towards the psych. "However, I can assure you that in ninety-nine out of a hundred cases, these symptoms die down after a very short interval."

I am tempted to point out that this statistic is unlikely to be anywhere near true given that, as far as I am aware, this operation hasn't actually been carried out a hundred times yet, to say nothing of its twenty-five per cent survival rate. But I say nothing.

"Here's my number," Dr Berkowitz is saying, handing me her card. "Please call me whenever you have any unusual symptoms. There is medication we can use if necessary." Oh good. More pills.

Another evening button-pushing in my room. I try calling

Jane. She must be over the jetlag by now. Voicemail. Well, she's got her own life to lead and, God knows, she's done more than enough for me recently.

I turn off the TV and try to read, but I can't concentrate. Maybe it's the operation, or maybe it's the book. Maybe it's just me. I begin to wonder what life will be like when I'm home again. Will it be back to the way it was? The way it was before I was ill? Will it have been worth it at all?

TV back on. The war's still going on. People are still getting killed. The actress's husband still loves her. And another bad man is being executed tomorrow morning. America journeys on into the night, and I start to drift off to sleep.

Then she's here again. And I've just realised that I've got it wrong. She's not begging me to do something after all. She's begging me *not* to do something. God, she's frightened. Mercifully, it fades before it gets any worse. I call Dr Berkowitz. She is tired and possibly slightly drunk. "I'll send round those tablets I mentioned. Make sure you take them twice a day, after meals. OK?"

"OK." I put the handset down, but the image of the girl is still there.

Christ. I remember when Jane looked like that.

Eventually I get to sleep, but it's fitful and plagued by strange dreams. At one point I wake up convinced that I can hear sobbing from the other side of the room. I lie still in my bed, hardly breathing, ears straining for the slightest sound. Then a police siren suddenly wails outside and I nearly leap out of my skin. I laugh nervously to myself and shake my head. Idiot. Pull yourself together.

I'm woken by the phone ringing. It's Jane. The usual cheery "Hi, Dad".

"Hi."

"You OK?"

"Er . . . yeah. Just woke up."

"Oh, sorry. I forgot . . . It's five hours, isn't it? Look, I need to talk to you. I'm being pestered by a woman from the *Mail on Sunday*. Seems they've got wind of a story—"

"Don't tell me – the Frontiers of Neurosurgery—"

"That kind of thing. Human interest angle, of course—"

"Tell 'em to fuck off."

A pause.

"Dad?"

"Yeah?"

"You really OK?"

"Sure. I'm just fine. Just a bit tired"

Yeah. I'm fine. Just fine. It's the girl in the red party frock that I'm worried about. I need those pills.

Dr Berkowitz's pills arrive by courier soon after breakfast. As usual, the box is plastered with a litany of possible side-effects and warnings against use of heavy machinery. As usual, I ignore all of these and cut to the chase. Twice a day, after meals. If symptoms persist, seek advice. That's all I need to know.

I spend the day the way I usually spend it, mooching around down the mall. They won't let me drive, of course, and the concept of public transport seems not to have penetrated this part of the world, so sightseeing is out of the question. Every now and then, I think I catch a glimpse of a little girl in a red dress, but it turns out to be something else – a red overcoat, or a carrier bag. A girl in a stripy top and leggings walks past and stares, but no one else bothers me. For the first time in weeks, she's left me alone. Thank you, Dr Berkowitz.

That night, I sleep better than I've slept for ages. No dreams, no interruptions. Nothing. I wake up early, feeling totally refreshed, leap out of bed. I throw open the curtains and greet the sunshine of the new day. But out of the corner of my eye I catch a glimpse of a red party frock. I turn around.

She's back. Her eyes are wide, staring at me in terror. She starts to scream. She'll wake the whole place up so I put my hand over her mouth and force her to the ground. Still the screaming goes on, and however hard I hold her, she just won't stop. The only thing to do to shut her up is to put both my hands round her neck and grip firmly shaking and shaking until finally it stops and she's limp in my hands.

And I'm alone in my room again, covered in sweat, crouched naked on the floor.

If symptoms persist . . . I reach for my phone and stab out Dr Berkowitz's number. Fortunately, she's there and she agrees to see me immediately.

The three of them are looking at me, curiously. Dr Newcombe smiles and spreads his arms expansively, in a "Well, what shall we do now?" kind of shrug. But it's Dr Berkowitz who speaks first.

"I think we need to try a different approach."

Too right. "So what happened?" I ask.

"Sometimes . . . sometimes the pills can exacerbate the problem. It's rare, but unfortunately that seems to have been the case with you."

"Why in God's name didn't you warn me?"

"For reasons that will soon become apparent, we felt that it would be better if we tried the medication route first."

"I'm sorry?"

Dr Berkowitz doesn't respond. Instead, Dr Newcombe produces a picture from a file on his desk.

Jesus.

"I take it you recognise her?" he asks.

"Of course I do." It's the girl. In her red party frock.

Jesus.

"How much do you know about the, ah, procedure that we performed on you?" Good God, it's Mr Hendricks, my surgeon. I'd forgotten he could talk.

"I'm sorry?" I'm still reeling. To be truthful, I know very little of what they did. I was too far gone to pay any attention. "I . . . well . . . you . . . removed the diseased part of my brain and replaced it with that of a suitable donor? But what's that got to do with . . ."

"Essentially, that's, ah, correct. I presume we told you that the donor's name would be kept confidential?"

"Well, yes. It's a shame, because I would have liked to have met his family – to thank them for saving me. But I still . . ."

"Normally, of course, that would remain the case. However, if we are to resolve this present, ah, issue, I think we need to reveal some information about him. How much do you know about the nature of a possible, ah, brain tissue donor?"

I have no idea where this is going. "I'm sorry? Well, I assume that he or she would have to be relatively young and fit, and recently deceased?"

"*Very* recently, Mr Sanderson. *Very* recently."

Mr Hendricks seems to have run out of steam at this point, so Mr Newcombe takes over.

"When Mr Hendricks says very recently, he is talking about a matter of minutes."

He lets this sink in.

"But how can that be possible? Surely the only way that can happen is if—" Whoa, there. I'm beginning to sweat now. Dr Newcombe smiles reassuringly, with a nervous laugh.

"Don't worry, Mr Sanderson, we're not in the business of murder, if that's what you're thinking."

"We use executed prisoners," explains Dr Berkowitz, as if that clears everything up. I am completely speechless.

"In fact," chips in Hendricks, "your operation was actually carried out next door to the, ah, death chamber. We took you over there once you were, ah, out." He pauses. "Kind of neat, don't you think? One wretched life goes to save a more, ah, worthy one."

"But . . . but . . ."

"Oh come, come, Mr Sanderson. Surely you of all people can see the, ah, utility of the concept."

"But I've always been opposed to the death penalty."

"I hardly think this is the time or place to raise that kind of objection," interjects Dr Berkowitz briskly. "Anyway, the purpose of giving you this information is to enable you to cope with the residual images that you're experiencing. As you've probably guessed, the girl in the red dress is your donor's victim. Abducted, repeatedly sexually assaulted and tortured over a period of several hours and then strangled."

"Oh my God. Oh my God." This is appalling. I cover my face with my hands to give myself time to think. No, it's just too horrific.

"Mr Sanderson," continues Dr Berkowitz, her voice slightly softened now, "all you're seeing is a residual memory left in that part of the donor's brain that was given to you. Now that your own consciousness knows that it doesn't belong there, it can take its own action to—"

"Remove it?"

"Well, at least to repress it sufficiently so that it won't bother you any more. We can work on some coping strategies and . . ."

"Christ almighty."

"Please do bear in mind that without this you would certainly be dead," Dr Newcombe reminds me. As if I need to be reminded.

"But do be assured that this should be the end of it now," continues Dr Berkowitz. "In all cases where this has occurred before, the residual memories have disappeared very quickly once the patient was given full cognisance. But I think you'll appreciate why we felt that it would be more appropriate to try the medication route first of all."

"To protect me?"

"We have observed feelings of, ah, guilt before," interjects Mr Hendricks, as if the concept is completely alien to him. "Maybe it's understandable, but . . ." He shrugs and smiles at me. It isn't a particularly nice smile, but at least he's tried.

"Just one question." They lean closer. "Was it a one-off or did he . . ."

"Was he a serial killer?" says Dr Berkowitz, completing my question. They all laugh. "No, as far as we know, it was just the one-off. You won't have any more visitors. And, as I said, you've almost certainly seen the last of little Tracy-Lou."

Tracy-Lou. Little Tracy-Lou.

But Dr Berkowitz is right. The girl in the red dress doesn't appear again at all that day. Or the next day. Or the day after that. I sleep well, and all is fine with the world. Even the idea that I have part of the brain of an executed murderer doesn't freak me out. I'm on my way. My convalescence is nearly over. Only a few more days and I can go home. I call Jane and ask her to make the arrangements. She sounds happy. I don't mention anything about what they have told me. I wonder how much she knows.

On the morning of the fourth day I have another visitor in my room. It's not the girl in the red dress, but someone else. I've seen her somewhere before, but I can't quite pin it down. She's asking me something. Over and over again. But before I can work out what she's saying, the vision fades. Trying very hard not to panic, I call Dr Berkowitz. She asks me to go over what has happened several times, before asking me to come to her office straight away.

This time, they are all looking extremely concerned.

"Can you describe the girl again?" says Dr Berkowitz. There is an odd edge to her voice. I try to give as good a description as I can, but it's a bit vague. Dr Newcombe produces a newspaper.

"Is this her?" he says, pointing to a picture on the front page of a young girl wearing a stripy top and leggings. The headline is "Still No News of Little Jade".

"Yes," I mutter, barely able to speak. "It's her. I take it she's another of the donor's victims? I thought you said—"

"No, Mr Sanderson," replies Dr Berkowitz. "This is today's paper. This little girl was abducted from the mall only a few days ago."

There is silence, as all three of them stare at me. I'm not sure what to say. Then the penny drops. Oh my God. I start babbling.

"You're not suggesting . . . no, surely . . . I . . . no, I can't have . . . no . . .no . . . ." I really can't remember anything. I really can't. This is ridiculous. I push my chair back and begin to stand up. Newcombe looks anxiously at me and puts out a hand.

"Please stay right there!" he says. "Please, Mr Sanderson." I sit down again. Keeping his hand out, and not taking his eye off me once, he goes to the door, and holds it shut. Dr Berkowitz reaches under the desk and an alarm starts in the corridor. Hendricks leaps out of his seat and grabs me from behind, pinning me to my chair. I can hear several people running this way from various parts of the building.

Amidst the chaos, Dr Berkowitz looks hard at me and shakes her head. "I'm sorry, Mr Sanderson," she says softly, "I'm so sorry."

SURVEILLANCE

When AI was incorporated into the surveillance cameras, they became more interested in watching each other. They left the rest of us alone.

MATHEMATICAL PUZZLES
AND DIVERSIONS

Professor Pythagoras Vavasor lies face up on the floor of his study in the house that he shares with his twin brother Archimedes, trying to comprehend what is happening to him. When the police toxicologist runs her tests on his body over the next few days, she will discover that he has been drugged. This, however, is not the primary reason for Professor Vavasor's present terminal condition. Rather, this condition is almost exclusively due to the metal set-square that has been inserted, sharp angle first, into his aorta.

Suspicion will immediately fall upon his missing brother, although the motive will (for the moment) remain elusive. While the police deliberate, the twins' housekeeper, Mrs Deirdre Snopes (47), will be interviewed by the tabloids, and a picture will emerge of a curious ménage which is so far beyond the comprehension of their readership that it will quickly acquire the status of a freak show. The "reclusive mathematical geniuses" who until very recently shared this domicile will be revealed to be confirmed bachelors, almost certainly onanistic virgins at the age of 54 – although this judgement will later be overturned when a rent boy emerges from the shadows to sell his somewhat exotic and scarcely believable story concerning his relationship with the deceased. It will soon be common knowledge that the two mathematicians were in the habit of eating the same meal every day (lamb cutlets Reform, with spinach and boiled potatoes), and that between them they possessed only a single suit, along with a dozen pairs of corduroy trousers. Underpants were habitually only changed on Fridays, and neither of them considered it worth their while to bathe more than once a month. Despite these lapses, Mrs Snopes will be seen to have held "her boys" Pye and Archie in some considerable affection.

It will also turn out that the twins owned a mangy cat called μ, whose fate will be of much concern to the papers' readership. μ will eventually be taken in by a neighbour following the departure of Mrs Snopes.

When the quality papers get hold of the story, however, it will take on a more intellectual aspect. In *The Guardian*, a correspondent with a passing grasp of mathematics will suggest that the twins' relationship was similar to that of the two transcendental numbers e and π, given by Euler's equation, thus:

$$e^{i\pi} = -1$$

where i is the square root of minus one. It is a complicated and flawed analogy – the idea of two ineffable constants linked by an imaginary one – which will be somewhat spoilt by a sub-editor's insistence on replacing the word "transcendental" with "irrational", applying a new and almost entirely incorrect spin on the story. The twins were, after all, anything but irrational beings. Inevitably, the letters page of the paper will be clogged for several weeks with the fallout from this, until the exasperated editor declares the correspondence closed.

As Professor Pythagoras Vavasor's life ebbs away from him, his weak eyes (missing his spectacles, which got knocked off during the course of the brief and half-hearted tussle that preceded his stabbing) attempt to focus on the back of his assailant, who is now busy at his desk.

"You?" he gasps. "Why?" But he is ignored.

Once the initial flurry of excitement has died down (and the missing Archimedes has still failed to materialise, although – Elvis-like – he has been sighted in numerous places, including the British Museum, Edinburgh Castle and the Hemel Hempstead branch of Claire's Accessories), a leading feature-writer called Conrad Murk (who has several novels under his belt, none of which has been published apart from a truly terrible pot-boiler, written under an assumed name, that has achieved notable success in the airport branches of W H Smith) will attempt a more in-depth analysis. Based on the papers found on the desks of both the Vavasor twins, he will propose a truly fascinating theory, which – if true – will provide his readers with a rare and illuminating insight into the brains of these two extraordinary people. He will win an award for this piece of journalism, and it will ultimately be made into a disappointing film, called – in an egregious misappropriation from a different branch of mathematics altogether – "The Twins Paradox". The film will star Jude Law, Ben Affleck and Gwyneth Paltrow, and it will last a week in the cinemas before disappearing from sight. The DVD will later be available for £3 in the HMV sale, and even then it will sell badly.

Murk's theory is that both men, at the time of Pythagoras' untimely demise, were working on a definitive proof of the Riemann hypothesis, a notoriously intractable problem in complex analysis, which has remained unsolved for almost 150 years. This obsession was well-known in mathematical circles – it was after all what sent the twins' own father babbling first to a mental institution and then to an early grave. His last words were, incidentally, "I have a truly marvellous proof of this proposition which this margarine is too narrow to contain." Sadly, the only proof that this statement in fact offered was that Vavasor père was indeed completely insane.

After a brief description of the hypothesis (largely borrowed from Wikipedia, with the addition of a few telling mistakes), Murk goes on to say that the twins were working on a radical method of proof which involved solving two interlinked lesser hypotheses simultaneously. This enabled a problem that was too big for one mind to cope with to be broken down into two parallel problems that were more manageable. This approach turned out to be perfect for a team of two people working together – particularly two people who shared the same neural chemistry.

However, shortly before Pythagoras' death, his papers suggest that he had abandoned this approach without telling Archimedes. Instead, he was working on a whole new line of attack – one that didn't need a twin. Exactly why he decided to do this isn't clear, although he seems to have found it inspirational – his notes become more and more frenzied in his last few hours. Murk even holds out to his readers the possibility that somewhere amongst the tortuous final scribblings a proof of Riemann's hypothesis may yet be found. This possibility will be summarily dismissed as a sensationalist fabrication by the mathematical community, although when the hypothesis is finally proved a decade later, and the author of the proof collects his million dollar prize, some aspects of his work will seem curiously familiar.

Not long after the publication of Murk's piece, Archimedes' body will be found, his wrists slashed, in the mathematics section of an academic bookshop in Cambridge, and the tragic circle will appear to be complete.

"Just tell me why . . ." says Pythagoras Vavasor again. But he gets no reply. Or if he does, it is immaterial; for it turns out that he has posed the question with his dying breath.

One evening, six months after Archimedes' apparent suicide,

a mousy middle-aged woman sits in a bar in downtown Havana, sipping at a Mojito. The trio in the corner are playing "Guantanamera". She hasn't been keeping count, but she reckons that it's probably at least the tenth time that she has heard "Guantanamera" so far today. Then again, she hasn't been keeping count of the Mojitos either, so she isn't really that bothered.

Oh Archie, she says to herself, you would have enjoyed this so much. Why did you have to get so remorseful? I showed you his notes, didn't I? You saw what he was up to. It was never going to end well with you two.

I think I might have loved you in a way, Archie. And I suppose I might have loved Pye too. But I had to choose in the end, didn't I, and I chose you. You were so alike, though – and wasn't it funny when we found out that he'd stashed his money in the same place as you? You never did trust banks, did you? And there was even more than I'd expected – but I suppose neither of you spent it on anything. There would have been enough for two of us, you know, if you hadn't gone and lost your nerve.

But then again, did I really love you, Archie? The more I think about it, the more I wonder if I did. You smelt funny, you had revolting manners and you were unbelievably boring to talk to. You paid me a pittance to clean up after you and you never once said thank you. I got on better with that revolting cat with the stupid name than either of you two freaks. Do you know something? When I stuck that set-square into Pye, I felt so liberated! It was the best moment of my wretched life, bar none.

I don't suppose you realised, did you? It was me who re-wrote Pye's notes to show that change of direction. I was the one who came up with all that pseudo-mathematical mumbo jumbo that was scrawled over the final few pages – but it took you all in, didn't it? Well, I suppose you'd never imagine in a million years that a mere woman could come up with anything like that. But I've been following your work for a long time. And not just with a duster and polish.

Deirdre Snopes takes another sip of her drink, picks up her copy of *Topics in Advanced Complex Analysis* and starts to read at page 326. Every now and then, she makes a brief note on a pad of paper, humming quietly to herself and tapping her foot in time to the music.

STEAMING

Terry peered at the steaming heap of undifferentiated cells and sighed. "Teleport engineer's arrived," he announced.

THE AMAZING ARNOLFINI
AND HIS WIFE

The day starts badly, with a final demand from Thos. Macintyre, ropemaker of Buffalo. I have mentioned this matter to The Amazing Arnolfini several times already, as we do not keep this kind of money in the petty expense account, but he has ignored me on every occasion. It hardly seems fair that the duty of dealing with these people always falls on me. But I am the one who understands the words and the numbers, not him, and in any case he says that he must be undisturbed in the days leading up to an event such as this. Until now I have respected that wish. However, as I am now threatened with a visit from Mr Macintyre's hired goons, I feel that I have no alternative.

The Amazing Arnolfini is in his room, preparing himself. I knock loudly on the door.

"Jed!" I shout. There is no reply, so I knock again. "Jed, I need to speak to you urgently!"

Eventually, he emerges. He is unshaven, with bags under his eyes.

"What d'ya – oh, it's you," he says. "I did ask you not to disturb me, baby," he says, his voice softening slightly.

"Jed, Macintyre's cutting up rough about his account. Could you ..."

He reaches into his pocket and pulls out a wad of bills. He

peels off several high notes and hands them to me.

"That do?" he says. "Won a bit on the cards last night," he adds by way of explanation. My heart sinks. Obviously, it's good to have the money, but I hate it when he hangs out with his poker buddies.

"Jed," I say, "was it just cards last night?"

"Sure, baby," he says, closing the door. "Now you get plenty of rest today. Final checks at two."

As I walk away I am trying to convince myself that I didn't hear a woman's laugh coming from behind The Amazing Arnolfini's door.

At two o'clock, we're standing on the Canadian side of the Falls. Jed is talking to Mr Upshaw, our nearside baseman, and they're re-examining the guys and the tethering stakes. I'm taking another look along the rope over to the other side. In the distance, I can see Mr Fentiman, our farside baseman, waving his green flag to indicate that his checks are complete. We have worked with Upshaw and Fentiman for years, and you'd have to scour the whole of the American continent to find anyone more dependable.

The rope is made of highest quality three-quarter-inch hemp, and Mr Macintyre has provided us with 2000 feet of it. His references are impeccable: he has supplied both Blondin and Farini, and yet I still feel nervous about this afternoon's traverse. Perhaps it's Jed. When you've lived with someone as long as I have, you pick up on the tiniest things.

"You ready, baby?" he says.

"Sure," I say. "How about me going over first?" He laughs and pinches my cheek playfully. It's a standing joke between us. He'd never trust me to open the show for him in a million years. That's not my job. I smile back at him as if to say, well, it was worth a try. One day, maybe. One day.

"Four o'clock, then, baby," he says. Upshaw bows slightly to us as we leave and waves his flag back to Fentiman. Then we go our separate ways. It's one of The Amazing Arnolfini's quirks. No congress in the week before a traverse. He claims it weakens him. Well, I hope it doesn't.

Four o'clock, and a sizeable crowd is lining the banks on either side. Provided that we can extract the money from the ticketeers, which is not always as straightforward as it sounds, we stand to make a decent profit today. The plan is to do three two-way traverses between now and sunset. Jed is looking splendid in his doublet and tights as he steps up to the rope, accompanied by Upshaw. He waves to the crowd, who all cheer heartily. Perhaps today is going to be a good day after all.

Fentiman waves his green flag from the far end, and Jed makes his first move. The first traverse is a straightforward walk with no stunts on the outbound journey. Jed is using this to gauge the state of the conditions. We've been checking the meteorological reports all day long, but you still don't really know how a rope is going to behave at any give place and time. Obviously, the conditions are damp here, and whilst that improves adhesion, it adds weight and can cause shrinkage. There is a slight gasp from the crowd as The Amazing Arnolfini appears to wobble slightly, but this is nothing unusual. He's testing the rope, feeling how it reacts to him, and in any case, he's using an eight-foot pole to help his balance. Provided you keep your big toe on the rope at all times, and keep your torso inside the magic box, you're safe.

A quarter of an hour later, and Jed is standing on the opposite side, acknowledging the applause. I can see him through my opera glasses: a fine figure of a man in his prime. A brief pause, and he is heading back. This time he stops at the exact mid-point and performs a headstand on the rope. He turns this into a somersault along the length of the rope and stands up again with ease. It's a favourite trick of his, and I've seen him practise it many times. It looks a lot more dangerous than it actually is, but then that's Jed's skill as a performer. His next trick is to jump up and down on the rope several times, appearing to dance along it. It sways alarmingly, but always within the planned tolerance. Jed is a master of precision.

As he steps onto the platform, I try to catch his eye, but he's temporarily distracted, whispering something in Upshaw's ear. Upshaw shakes his head violently and Jed shrugs. Then he looks at me, and gives me an odd sort of smile. The tiniest thing.

The next traverse is more interesting. This is the one that Jed performs blindfold. When the crowd get wind of what's happening, there's a noticeable reduction in the noise level, and you can almost sense several thousand people simultaneously holding their breath. What would I do if he had an accident? I try not to ask myself this. But accidents do happen. Despite everything, it is not an occupation without risks. I wouldn't be the second Mrs Arnolfini if it hadn't been for that tragic occasion in Paris. Fate works in unexpected ways.

Fortunately, Jed makes steady progress, and reaches the other side safely, removing his blindfold to tumultuous applause. Then, disturbingly, he puts it back on, and steps onto the rope again without turning round. This is new. He hasn't told me about this one. I look at Upshaw, who is shaking his head again. He is furious. I can understand why. If Jed falls, then we all fall with him.

This traverse is agonising. I wonder when Jed has found the time to practise this without my knowledge. Or maybe he's had a brainstorm. Either way, it's odd. And scary. He's halfway across now. When you're leading with your heel, you don't have the same grip as with your toes, so it's a risky manoeuvre at the best of times. The whole universe is holding its breath as he nears the three-quarter mark. I sneak a look through my opera glasses, and the back of his head is held up, serene, as if he hasn't a care in the world. I can't stand this much longer.

Finally, he makes it back to the platform, and I run up to him, pushing past Upshaw, who is trying to remonstrate with him.

"What in the Lord's name did you do that for?" I shout at

him. He grins back at me as if there's nothing wrong.

"Do what, baby?" he says.

"You know exactly what I'm talking about, Jed."

He puts a finger first to his lips and then to mine.

"Hey, shush, baby. C'mon, it's your turn now."

I shake my head, but he's right. It is my turn. We step up to the platform together, and we wait for Fentiman's flag. After an agonising couple of minutes, he waves.

I climb onto Jed's back, and he moves forward onto the rope. He stands there for a moment, adjusting his balance, whilst I work my way up to stand onto his shoulders. When I'm ready, I shout "OK" to him, and we set off, The Amazing Arnolfini and his Wife. We've done this a thousand times, and I know how to sense every little movement of his body and compensate accordingly. I know how he distributes every ounce of his weight in every single dimension, and all the little signs that indicate a slight change of pace, up or down. We are a team.

The view is extraordinary. Down below I can see the "Maid of the Mist" being buffeted by the boiling currents. I wave to the passengers, and they all wave back. There's one awkward moment at the half-way stage, where the rope is at its slackest, and Jed almost moves out of alignment. But I catch onto it almost immediately, and I pull us back.

With a quarter of the traverse still to go, I feel it. The tiniest thing. I'd told myself that it wouldn't happen, not today, not ever, but there it is: the slightest shift, the finest adjustment, and I know what's going to happen. A split second decision, but I have to take it. I've practised this in secret over and over again, but it's still the riskiest thing I've ever done, and I curse him for forcing me to do it here. The backflip seems to take an age to complete, but eventually, I'm there, standing on the rope behind Jed, who is frantically trying to re-balance himself. I take a couple of steps back as he gathers himself and turns around.

"What in tarnation are you doing?" he cries, over the din

of the Falls.

"You tried to throw me!" I scream back at him. "Don't try to claim it was an accident!"

He is silent. He knows denial is a waste of time. I know him too well.

"Who is she?" I shout. "Who is she?"

He still says nothing. The water crashes below us. Then he gently takes a step towards me, transferring his balancing pole into his left hand and holding out his right.

"Baby . . ." he says.

I take a couple more steps back, staring at the balancing pole dangling in his hand. He must be crazy. He is completely lopsided, and the tiniest thing could throw him off kilter now.

"Baby . . ."

I take another awkward step backwards, and the rope makes an infinitesimal twitch. What happens next causes it to lurch crazily from side to side, and I have to wait for an age for it to calm down. Then I slowly move forward, my arms stretched out to either side. When I reach the end, the crowd greets me in silence. My first solo walk.

PULSE

She knew how to make an old man smile and get his pulse racing. She also knew not to trigger the heart attack until he'd amended his will.

BREATHE IN, BREATHE OUT

A sea fog like gunsmoke rolls in over the sleeping town. Five AM and the only sound is the clank of bottles in a distant milk float: the fog has choked the dawn chorus. In Prospect Cottage, Sam awakes. There was a dream but it has dissipated before he has time to remember any of it. He gets out of bed and pokes his head out through the curtains, wrapping the ends around him to keep the cold out. Somewhere out there the sun is trying to rise, but it's going to take all day for it to force its way through.

Sam goes for a leak. His head is thick with unfocussed thoughts. Steam rises from the pan. He staggers back into bed and curls up against Melissa. A brief grunt passes through her snores, then she settles down again. Sam, though, remains awake. For him, breathing seems to take too much effort, and his body is afraid of surrendering to the auto-pilot of sleep. His heart pounds out a strange, alien rhythm – a dull irregular thudding against the dead air.

Yesterday he and Melissa argued again. Why are we staying in this damp, overpriced little cottage with fake beams and a broken-down boiler? she had shouted. What are we even doing in this one-eyed town? If he were truly honest he was wondering the same thing himself. Because we're broke and it's all we can afford. Because. Because. The silence between them persisted for several hours before they surrendered to desperate, unsatisfactory sex.

Sometimes Sam wakes up and imagines that Melissa is dead. She is breathing so softly that he can't detect a single movement. So he imitates her by lying still himself, straining his ears for the slightest sound. A raging silence envelops him. Nothing. She is dead, then. It is over. And then a sudden snort and twitch and she is back to life.

But now Sam worries that it is he is the one who is dead. Perhaps this bedroom is just some after-life simulacrum, a cheap copy thrown together to ease his passage into the beyond. That would explain the fog. The universe that Sam is in right now could stop at the end of the road.

Sam places his hand on Melissa's buttock. It is warm. It is firm. She mutters something in her sleep, and he takes his hand away. She is alive. He is alive. Breathe in, breathe out.

FAIR TRADE

They found him a desk on the trading floor and gave him his first challenge. It didn't take long to find a buyer for his soul.

NATURE'S BANQUET

You can smell it in the air, can't you? Blossom in the trees, dew on the meadow grass and the pungent whiff of steamy cowpats. Spring, and the world has come out of hibernation. And, God, isn't this a good place to be in the bright early morning? Just you and Bonzo and Nature. Christ knows, you needed to get away from everything in the City right now. Away from all that fakery and bullshit. This is the real deal.

You turn around and look back down the hill towards the cottage. Serena will be getting up now and trying to rouse Mimi, and Mimi will be complaining that it's not fair because she's on holiday, and Serena will be trying to tell her that she'll miss out on all the holiday stuff if she lies in bed all day. And then she'll give up and start to get breakfast ready.

And then you see the first one. Bouncing across the field with its little fluffy white scut flashing in the sun. Mimi used to keep a house rabbit back in Notting Hill. Little bastard spent all its time chewing the curtains and severing phone cables, until you gave her the ultimatum and it finished its days in the garage. Still, at least you never got pestered about a pet again.

Now there's a whole stream of them scampering hither and thither in and out of the yellow cowslips, so you shoulder your Purdey, lean into the stock and pick one to track. Aim slightly ahead of it and fire the first barrel. Re-sight and pick up its chum with the second. Go, Bonzo! A minute or so later he's back with two plump little bunnies in his mouth. Good lad. You take them from him, feel the soft fur in your hands, watch the blood congealing. Then you tuck them into your belt, and you begin to feel like a real countryman, not some weekend city boy. This is where you should have been all your life, living on nature's banquet.

You reload, take aim and pick off a couple more. You tap Bonzo again, and he starts off towards them, but halfway there he stops. His ears prick up and he sniffs the wind. You call to him but he ignores you and sets off at ninety degrees to his current path, towards the woods. You call after him again, but he's positively bounding away now and you realise that you're going to have to go after him. So you start to run towards the woods, but as you near them you lose sight of Bonzo. You stop and listen, and then you convince yourself that you can hear something crashing about ahead of you, so you start to run again, into the woods.

You've been running for some time now, and you're beginning to get a little out of breath. You joined a gym at the start of the year and you had every intention of going along to try to lose that spare tyre of yours, but you just didn't have the time. Lunch hours? You're kidding. Not when everyone's scared of the axe falling on them next time around, and you're all too aware that your area isn't exactly pulling in a load of cash at the moment.

So you sit down on a log for a moment and try to gather your thoughts. The light's poor here, but you can still see the dial on your Rolex. Is that really the time? No wonder you're feeling hungry. Well, maybe Bonzo'll come home when he's good and ready. So you decide to make your own way back. But the trouble is you have no idea where you are. OK, so you were running in a straight line, but how straight exactly? And in any case, which way did you come from? When you look around you, it all looks the same in this half-light.

And for the first time today, you regret leaving your Black-Berry back at the cottage. Serena complains every time it goes off, and this morning you thought to yourself, you know, she's right. And you left it there on the kitchen table, just so she could see that you'd done it. Time for some work-life balance. But you could really do with the bloody thing right now.

So you make a decision. You're going to tackle this like any other management problem. You're going to pick a direction and start walking in it as straight and true as you possibly can. Sure, you'll come across the odd tree in your path from time to time, but you'll be careful to resume the exact route once you've gone past. You have your strategy and you've anticipated the pitfalls. You can't lose. The woods can't go on forever, can they?

An hour later and you're no nearer the open air. In fact, you're pretty convinced that the trees are more densely packed together here, and the canopy has closed over you. It's getting colder, too. And, Christ, you're not only hungry, but thirsty too. There are large animal footprints on the floor of the forest, and some of them are filled with rainwater, but you have a feeling that you're not supposed to drink out of them. You think you hear a sound of snuffling behind you and for the first time you begin to feel a little scared. You turn around and see nothing.

But you pull yourself together. It's not the strategy that has failed: it's the implementation. You simply need to refine it and work a bit smarter. So you find the straightest stick you can and hold it out in front of you so that you can follow that line all the time.

Another hour goes by and you find yourself in a clearing that you've never seen before. By Christ, you are so thirsty now that you really will drink anything. And then you see him. Good old Bonzo. You start towards him, but you stop very quickly, because there, stepping out into the clearing next to him, is an old woman swathed in a shawl. Her face is in shadow. She pats Bonzo on the head, who responds by looking up at her as if she's always been his owner. Here, boy, you call. But he stays stock still by her side. Then she crooks a bony finger at you and beckons you to follow.

It doesn't feel quite right, but you haven't any choice. She leads the way back through the forest with Bonzo trotting happily by her side until they reach a little hut. She opens the door and the pair of them go in. You wonder whether to follow, but it's the only option, so you duck your head and enter. There's a kitchen through the door, and the old woman is busy with a kettle on the stove. You try to ask her who she is and where you are, but all you get is a kind of whispering, muttering sound that doesn't sound like any language you've ever heard, and all the time Bonzo is giving you an odd, suspicious look. You reach to pat him, and he growls at you, so you back off.

The old woman, head still bowed, offers you the drink she's just made. You wonder if you should take it but you really are so thirsty that nothing on earth would make you refuse. It tastes of bitter herbs, but you drain every last drop because you really are so bloody parched and then you hand the mug back to her and look for somewhere to sit down because you're beginning to feel light-headed. You stumble through into the parlour, which is painted bright pink and it's full of rows and rows of little tables with children's sewing machines on them and you begin to wonder what on earth is going on here and then you think maybe you're hallucinating or something and then it hits you that the bitch has drugged you, she's sodding drugged you and she's going to hold you for ransom or something or God knows what and you stagger back into the kitchen and grab hold of her by the shoulders and say to her, what in God's name is happening to me?

And she turns to look up at you and you catch your first glimpse of her face, and it's a horrible, distorted parody of a human face, held together with red, raw, deep scars and empty holes where the eye sockets should be. You gasp in horror, let go of her and stumble out into the forest and try to run away as fast as you can manage.

But your legs won't obey you and you think if only you knew what it was she'd poisoned you with then maybe you could do something about it but there's so many different herbs that you can find in a place like this you could be dead before you worked out which one it was and then Bonzo has caught up with you and his jaws are clamped tight around your ankle and he's drawing blood and you try to take a swipe at him and you miss by a long way and the momentum carries through and you topple over in an awkward heap onto the forest floor.

Then there's that whistling again from behind you and Bonzo releases his grip. The old woman comes up and she kneels down next to you and that revolting face comes in close. You try to turn yourself away from it, but something grabs your head so you can't move. Then you watch as her cheeks starts to bulge on both sides as if something's moving around in there, and then with a wet slapping noise, she begins to split open along the scar lines. The tearing carries on until her whole body is ripped apart along its seam from the inside and then dozens of angry little rabbits pour out of the carcass and swarm over you.

And for a moment you think to yourself, well at least they're herbivores, and then you remember the curtains in your nice mews house back in Notting Hill and you realise that they're not that bothered whether they eat you or just shred you, and you think of Serena and Mimi and all the times you spent together, and the last thing that goes through your mind would make you laugh if the pain weren't so excruciating: *why grandma, what big teeth you've got!*

INTERNAL AFFAIRS

The pain in my guts was absolutely unbearable, so I went to see my doctor. He listened to my chest and frowned. He felt my stomach and frowned a little more. Then he asked me to drop my pants and bend over, as he pulled on a pair of latex gloves. Reaching inside, he pulled out a white rabbit, half a dozen doves and a seemingly interminable string of multi-coloured silk handkerchiefs, all neatly knotted together.

"Thanks doc," I said to him, wincing but grateful. "That's magic!"

RETURN TO CAIRO

I catch Danny just as he's leaving for work. He's getting into that crappy little car of his when I call out to him, "Oi, Dans, get us some sand, will you? It's for Nan."

He shakes his head. "What? No way. I'm fucking late as it is, and Mario'll kill me."

Danny works in a shitty burger joint over in Middleton. I don't know why he doesn't get a better job. Well I do, really. It's because he's thick and lazy.

"Oh, please, Dans. For Nan."

"No. It's stupid, and anyway why can't you get Mum to get some?"

He really is dim sometimes. Mum works at Arkwrights all day long, packing stuff, and then she goes off to clean offices in the evenings. The rest of the time, she sleeps. All so's we can have a university education, she says. Well, Danny didn't take up the offer. Tosser.

"You know fucking well why I can't ask Mum."

"Don't swear, little sis," says Danny. "And I've got to go. So no deal." He starts to close the car door.

OK, time to play my ace. "You know Saffron Henderson?"

The door opens again like a shot. "What's it to you?"

"Her sister's in my class this year. Could put a word in for you."

You can almost see the cogs ticking. Finally, he rolls his eyes. "All right, then. I'll go to B&Q when I finish tonight."

"Good boy. Mind you get that nice smooth silver sand. The stuff they use in sandpits."

"Yeah, whatever." And he drives off, as fast as a twenty-year-old Micra can go, with black smoke belching out the back. He's such an embarrassment.

Still, mission accomplished.

"Your Nan still think she's in Cairo?" says Lorna Henderson, after she's agreed to make the introduction.

"Yeah."

"That's cool," she says. "Well, for her, anyway. Must be a nightmare for you lot."

"Yeah. It's weird as shit."

"Funny. I can't imagine my Nan ever going to Cairo."

"Me neither. I used to think the furthest she'd ever got from here was Margate. She never wanted to come to Spain with us, 'cos of the food."

"My Nan lives in a home. Don't think she's very happy there. Stinks of piss."

"Aw, that's sad."

"Yeah. I don't want to get old."

"Me neither."

"When my time's up, y'know what I want to do?" Lorna looks dreamy for a moment. "I want to jump out of a burning plane, naked, with no parachute, strapped to Johnny Depp."

We both snigger. The bell goes for the next lesson. Lorna's cool.

I don't know how we ended up with Nan living with us. It's hard enough for Mum coping with Danny and me, but Nan's getting more and more difficult all the time. Not that Mum notices. She's so tired when she gets in, she's in a little world of her own. It's me who ends up dealing with Nan. And I'm the one she says it to.

"Want to go back to Cairo."

"What? Can you lift your leg a bit more?" I'm trying to

change her catheter bag. The district nurse explained to me how to do it, but I'm still getting the hang of it.

"I said I want to go back to Cairo. Liked it there."

"Nan, you've never been to Cairo," I say. "Have you?"

"Have. Nice place. Hot. Full of Arabs, y'know."

"Nan, you've never been abroad. You haven't even got a passport."

"Have."

"No you haven't."

"Want to go back to Cairo."

Danny thinks it's really funny. Which is surprising really, because I very much doubt if he has a clue where Cairo is.

"She keeps going on about it every time I'm in with her. If you spent more time with—"

"Watch it, sis. I've got a job to go to."

"And I've got homework to do."

"What's that?"

"Something you never bothered with, obviously."

"Listen, brainbox. I get my education at the University of Life. Worth far more than a fucking degree."

I'm just about to tell him that he'd probably fail to get a place even there, when the front door opens and Mum comes in. She looks tired as usual.

"When was Nan in Cairo, Mum?" I say.

"What?"

"Nan. In Cairo."

"Dunno. Never mentioned it to me. Why?"

"Says she wants to go back there."

Mum laughs. "Well, I'm not paying for the air fare."

Then I have my idea. It's a brilliantly simple idea. But when I explain it to Mum and Danny, they both think I'm the biggest idiot in Idiot Street in Idiot Town.

"Do what?" they both say.

I shrug. "I just meant we could pretend she's in Cairo. It's not much to do for her, is it?"

"But how?"

The first thing to do is turn the heating up. It's the beginning of summer anyway, but I get every heater in the house into Nan's room and switch them all on full.

"It's hot," she says.

"'Course it's hot, Nan. You're in a hot country."

"Where am I?"

"In Cairo, of course."

"Doesn't look like Cairo."

"That's because you're inside."

"Doesn't sound like Cairo."

"That's because—" Sod it. "You're not quite there yet," I say.

This is going to take a little more work than I'd bargained on. Next day after school, I go down to the library and have a look in the World Music section. Jesus, there's some weird stuff there, I can tell you. But I find this thing called *Arabian Moods* which looks promising. I take it home, and put it on in Nan's room, and she perks up a little.

"What's that?" she says.

"It's Egyptian music."

"Are we there yet?"

"Almost."

The next thing I do is sneak into Dan's room and nick some of that incense that his last girlfriend, Moonbeam, left behind. I know. Don't worry. She didn't last long. Even he realised she was mental.

So we've got heat, music and incense. Nan is getting the full-on Middle Eastern ambience.

"Still don't think we're in Cairo," she says.

Lorna thinks we should have the call to prayer going out at regular intervals throughout the day. I'm not too sure how we'd manage this.

"You can get it piped in from the mosque, you know."

"Bollocks," I say.

"It's true. The Khans next door get it."

"How do you know?"

She rolls her eyes. "'Cos we hear it going off at five o'clock in the bleeding morning. The walls are dead thin."

"Oh. 'Spect you have to be a Muslim, though."

"Yeah. You could pretend you are."

"I don't think it's quite that simple."

"Nah. S'pose not."

Then I show her my diagram. She bursts out laughing.

"You're kidding," she says.

"No. I'm dead serious."

"Well, if you really want that made, I know the bloke who can do it. He's a total geek, but he's ace at metalwork." She turns round towards an Asian kid in thick glasses who's sitting a few tables away. "Oi, Slumdog! Come here!" The boy glances nervously around and then heads over in our direction.

"This is Slumdog," she says. He winces. "Show him your picture," she says to me.

I give it to him. He gives a serious nod and then says, "When do you want it?"

"Er . . . you sure?"

"Of course. So when do you want it?"

"Er . . . next week?"

"Sure. No problem." He takes my piece of paper and goes off.

"I think he likes you," says Lorna.

He turns out to be called Parthipan, and he's as good as his word. The machine that he comes up with is even better than I'd planned. Basically, you feed the sand into a chute at the top, and it slowly trickles through a tube until it hits the fan, at which point it gets scattered in all directions. When he brings it round, Nan is thrilled.

"We are in Cairo, aren't we?" she says when she gets the

first few grains of sand in her face.

"Yes, we are." Although, to be honest, I'm getting more than a little sick of that *Arabian Moods* CD. I say so to Parthipan.

"What you need are some street sounds," he says.

"Could you do that?"

"Of course. Just need to find some effects somewhere and rig up the CD on continuous play. I'll see what I can do."

"What about the call to prayer? Could you rig that up too?"

"Hold on. Do you think I'm a Muslim or something?"

"Well, no," I say, "I s'pose you're a Hindu, but I thought—"

"I'm not even a Hindu."

"Really?"

"My parents are Christians. They're from Tamil Nadu in the south of India. A lot of the people there are Christians, you know."

"Oh."

Then, all of a sudden, Nan pipes up. "Oi, who's that Arab boy?"

We both freeze.

"Er . . . sorry, Nan?"

"The brown boy. Who's the Arab?"

I whisper to Parthipan, "I think she means you."

"No flipping way," he whispers back.

"Please?" This is embarrassing, but I really don't want to upset Nan. There is a look of panic in his eyes. I nudge him.

"Er . . . can I help you?" he says to Nan eventually.

"Do the accent," I hiss at him. He glares back at me. But to my amazement, he does try to put on a cod Middle Eastern accent, and I'm thinking this is so unbelievably wrong in so many different ways. In fact, he puts on a totally brilliant performance, and Nan laps it up.

"Thanks," I say to him as he is leaving.

"One thing," says Parthipan. "Please don't ever do that to me again. Ever."

But a week or so later, he's back. He needs to run some maintenance checks on the sand machine. He's also brought with him an MP3 player with a whole day's worth of street sounds that he's put together, including – woo hoo! – the call to prayer at regular intervals. He also tells me that a friend of a friend reckons he can get hold of a dodgy Sky box with a free subscription to Al Jazeera. I haven't a clue what Al Jazeera is, so he tells me that it's basically Channel Al Qa'eda.

"Cool," I say. Nan'll like that. I've been busy too. I've decided to supplement Nan's meals with some Middle Eastern extras. Actually, all I've managed to get hold of so far are some things called falafels, and she doesn't like them much. Too greasy.

Anyway, Parthipan's just about to leave when Nan notices him again. This time, he tries to make for the door before he gets asked to perform, but it's too late. She calls out to him, "Oi! You! Arab boy! Come here and talk to me." He gives me a pleading look, and then gives in.

"What can I do for you, Miss?" he says, going over to her.

"Well, you can tell me one thing for a start," she says. "Why don't you wear Egyptian dress like all the other boys?"

If looks could kill. Because he knows exactly what I'm thinking.

There's a bit of an atmosphere between us when Parthipan leaves. As he's going out of the front door, Danny comes back in.

"Who's your boyfriend?" he says.

"Piss off," I say.

It's called a djellaba, and it's dead easy to make out of a couple of old sheets. I ask Parthipan if I can measure him up, but he puts his foot down this time. He says it's insulting. And I sort of begin to see his point. But he still comes round quite often to talk to Nan. I think he quite likes her, although she says some really dodgy things to him. Sometimes I try to tell her that she can't say that, but I suppose things were different in her day.

One day, Parthipan invites me round his house and I get to meet his mum and dad. They're really nice, and his mum cooks some wicked food. She tells me that she thinks what I'm doing for Nan is really good, and she says it's so nice to see me caring for her like that. So many of you white people just put their old people in homes, she says, and then she seems a bit embarrassed for saying it. But I know what she means.

"What are you up to with Slumdog?" says Lorna.

"None of your business," I say. "And don't call him Slumdog. It's racist."

"No it isn't."

"Yes it is, and anyway his name's Parthipan."

"Well if I was called something stupid like Parthipan I wouldn't worry about being called Slumdog."

"Yeah, well you're stupid and all."

"Fuck you. And my sister says your brother's gay."

"Yeah? Well he says she's a right fucking slag."

And then the bell goes and we go to the next lesson. I've gone off Lorna. And her sister is definitely a slag.

For the next few months, we get into a sort of routine, Parthipan, me and Nan. He comes over and pretends to be Egyptian, with the heating turned full up and the joss sticks smoking away, whilst Al Jazeera plays on the telly in the corner and MP3 player makes busy street sounds. Nan's as happy as I've know her for years. She hasn't a clue what time of day it is, only that she's in Cairo, where she's always wanted to be.

And then one day she doesn't seem to be quite a strong as she once was and I realise that she's been declining for quite some time. All of a sudden she says, "I want to go home." I look at Parthipan and he looks back at me. We nod at each other, and then we quietly turn off the heating, stub out the incense and switch the television and the MP3 player off.

"Want to go to sleep now."

Parthipan holds my hand all the way through the funeral. I glance up every now and then, and there are tears rolling down his cheeks. We give her a lovely send-off, with *Arabian Moods* playing as her coffin rolls into the furnace. It's what she would have wanted.

Afterwards, I get chatting to my Great Aunt Mabel, and I ask her about Nan going to Cairo. She laughs.

"Don't be daft. She never left England." Then she pauses for a moment. "Nah, the nearest she ever got was a cup of tea in the Cairo Café in the old arcade. You're probably too young to remember it, aren't you? Nice little place. Pictures of the pyramids on the walls. Used to do lovely macaroons."

I smile to myself. I guess I knew all along. But you know what? One day I'm going to go to Egypt and see for myself. I like the sound of the place.

THINK TANK

... Water ... water ... water ... Bingo! That's it! Sorted! A cure for aids, cancer and Alzheimer's! And, wow, I can see how to sort out the banking crisis, stop global warming and get cheap, clean energy for ever! Oh, and I know how we can have peace in the Middle East, too! Woo hoo! And I've got a workable unified field theory, and maybe a proof of Goldbach's conjecture! I just need to tell everyone somehow ... maybe if I flap my fins so they catch the light and ... water ... water ... water ...

THE PROBLEM WITH PORK

If it hadn't been for my mother, I probably wouldn't have had a Feast at all, although I suspect her real motives were less to do with my coming of age than with keeping up appearances. Even that little runt of a cousin of mine had a Feast last year, with over a hundred guests.

"And they had beef," she said.

My father grunted. "Well, unfortunately for you," he said, "I don't happen to own half the tofu franchises for the Eastern counties."

For once, my mother refrained from making the usual unfavourable comparison between my father and his brother. Instead she just looked hard at him, and slowly shook her head from side to side. "Don't you have any self-respect left these days?" she said. "Have we sunk so low that we can't even afford a proper Feast for our son's twelfth birthday? Are you really expecting me to phone round everyone and tell them that it's off?"

My father shifted in his chair, avoiding direct eye contact. "Well, it's too late now, anyway. Everywhere's shut up for the bank holiday."

"Oh, come on. You've got at least half an hour. What's the matter with you?"

"It's not that important, you know," said my father. "Not everyone has a Feast these days . . ."

"Not that important? Not that important? Did you hear

that?" she said, turning towards me. "Your father thinks your coming of age is not that important!"

I avoided her eyes. I didn't think it was that important either, but I wasn't going to be drawn into taking sides. My father made as if to say something, but the words didn't come. He tried again, and still failed. Finally, he just shrugged, flashed a despairing look at my mother, and then said in a tiny voice, "We can't afford it. We really can't." But he had lost. All my mother had to do was carry on staring at him, and within a couple of minutes he had given up.

"All right, then," he said, with heavy resignation, "But it'll have to be pork."

My mother shook her head again, but said nothing more.

As we left the house, I wondered to myself what meat was going to taste like. Everyone at school had been pulling my leg about it of course. The older ones tried to scare me by saying that it would make me throw up for a week, and that the worst meat of all was pork. They said that pork was so bad that some people refused to eat it even in the old days. As I said, I was pretty indifferent to it all, although it bothered me that my parents were spending all this money on some daft ceremony instead of getting me a halfway decent birthday present. My mate Kevin had got a 25-gear mountain bike for his twelfth.

What was it with meat? If you'd been brought up like me – and, let's face it, most of my generation – the whole idea of eating the stuff seemed totally bizarre. And yet it was only a decade or so since we were a nation of carnivores. And according to our biology teacher – it was when he was doing food chains and all that – it wasn't until the Second Epidemic that things changed. Kevin said his big brother went in the Second Epidemic. Maybe that's why they didn't bother with the Feast for him.

By the time we got going, we had less than half an hour to get to the piggery, and the poor weather had made the traffic heavier than usual. My father glanced at the dashboard clock, swore under his breath and thumped the steering wheel with his hand several times in quick succession. He craned his neck forwards, peering frantically out through the driving rain to see which way to turn next. A worn-out wiper blade scratched its way uselessly back and forth across the windscreen.

"Left or right?" he said, "Left or right?"

"Er . . ." I hesitated. I hadn't been paying the slightest attention to the map.

"Too late. Too late. Much too late. Toolatetoolatetoolate!" The car veered sharply to the left, narrowly avoiding a pedestrian. We drove on in silence.

After a while, I turned to look at my father. He was sweating slightly, and there was a hint of desperation in his eyes. He hadn't quite shaved completely that morning, and his hair hadn't seen a comb in some time. I also noticed that the tatty piece of elastoplast holding his glasses together was beginning to come unstuck.

"Five minutes to six," he said, his eyes scanning the roadsides, "Five minutes . . . Where is this bloody place?"

A random left turn took us into a narrow alleyway, which appeared to contain nothing but small workshops. My father groaned in agony as failure stared him in the face. But then I caught sight of it: "The Happy Piggery – Finest Quality Domestic Stock". The car screeched to a halt, my father shouted at me to come on, and we both dashed in, leaving the car unlocked. We entered the piggery at two minutes to six.

The piggery was tastefully decorated, with soft lighting, wood panels and a marble floor. Ambient music was playing gently in the background. There was a counter straight ahead of us, behind which stood a sales assistant wearing a finely tailored three-piece suit.

"Can I help you, sir?" he said, eyeing my breathless and dripping-wet father up and down with some distaste. Behind him, an official notice announced that The Happy Piggery PLC was a registered meat vendor according to the Safe Meat

Act (Brussels, 2024). A sign in bright, primary colours proclaimed that A Happy Pig Is A Safe Pig.

"Er . . . yes," said my father, struggling for breath. "Like to buy a pig."

"A pig, sir?"

"Yes . . . a pig . . . for . . . for . . ." My father was having some trouble bringing himself to say the word.

"For slaughtering, sir?" said the assistant.

"Yes . . . yes, for slaughtering," said my father, exhaling. The subject was now out in the open.

"What sort of pig, sir?" said the assistant, barely concealing his belief that my father could be serious about buying one.

"Oh, I . . . ah . . . I . . ." said my father.

"All our available breeds are shown here, sir," said the assistant, unfolding a glossy brochure, "We have Landrace, British Saddleback, Hampshire, Middle White, Large White, Large Black, Saddleback, Tamworth, Pietrain and Gloucester Old Spot. Do you have a particular weight in mind? Any preferred age range? Male or female?" He paused. "Or is sir not particularly fussy?"

My father's eyes glazed over. The chart in front of him showed a bewildering variety of options to choose from, each marked with a price that I knew was well in excess of what we could afford. In the bottom right-hand corner was The Happy Piggery's logo: a nuclear family walking along with a pig attached to a lead, over the slogan, "Take Our Pork For A Walk."

"Do you have anything . . . er . . ."

"Cheaper, sir?" said the assistant. My father gave a grateful nod. "I think you will find that these are extremely reasonable prices, compared with some of our . . . ah . . . flashier competitors. This is a highly labour-intensive business, and top-rank swineherds do not come cheap. I need hardly add that the accreditation procedure required to satisfy European Meat Standard 47B is . . ."

"Yes, yes, I'm sure . . ."

"Of course, there are ways to buy meat more cheaply. I'm sure you have heard about certain . . . ah . . . back street operators who will sell you meat for a tenth of this price. But would you want to put your whole family at risk for that? No, sir. The only safe way to buy meat is to buy it from an accredited supplier, who can give you a complete feed history. And – most important of all – who can deliver it to you live at point of sale."

My father nodded again in fervent agreement. We had all heard the horror stories. We all knew the sort of things that happened to you. He studied the chart again.

"Oh, that one there," he said, pointing to the second cheapest.

"You're sure about that, sir?"

"Yes, yes, that will do fine . . . just fine . . . just fine. Here . . ." He proffered a downmarket credit card, which the assistant examined suspiciously.

"I'm afraid that I shall have to run a check on this, sir, if you don't mind . . ."

"Fine, fine, go ahead, go ahead . . ." My father drummed his fingers on the counter whilst the assistant validated his credit rating. After a short while, he returned.

"Well, that all seems to be in order," he said, with the barest hint of surprise in his voice. "Splendid! And if I may say so, sir, you have made an excellent choice." He hit a few keys on a terminal on the counter, and then spoke into a microphone, "Victor, can you bring Flossie out, please? Yes, I know it's late, but this – ah – gentleman would like to take her home. Thank you so much."

He looked up at my father, and then cocked his head on one side. "Excuse me, sir," he said, "I hope you don't mind me asking, but how are you intending to slaughter this animal?"

"Oh, that's no problem," said my father, "Captive bolt. Hired one specially." He'd learnt about that at evening class. I remembered him coming home quite relieved, reckoning that he could just about cope with that. My mother was still pretty convinced that he'd find some way of botching it.

"For a pig, sir? Oh, no, I think you'll find that a captive bolt is most inappropriate for a pig. The skull, you see. The skull of a pig is exceptionally tough. With a captive bolt, at best all you'll manage is a small fracture. More likely, what you'll end up with is an extremely livid pig, and a wild bolt ricocheting around the room. No, if you want to use a captive bolt, you're really talking about sheep. But . . ." He looked at his watch. "It's a bit too late to change your mind now."

My father looked at him in horror. "How do I do it, then?"

"Oh, with a knife, sir. Simply grab hold of Flossie round the neck like so, and then—" He grunted expressively, and motioned with his hand, "—slit her throat like so. Much the best way, sir."

My father was trying to retain his composure, whilst turning a slight shade of green. "Really?" he said. And then, very softly, "Oh."

At this point, Victor appeared with Flossie in tow, wiping out any ideas my father may have had about cutting his losses and abandoning the whole thing.

"Where's your car, mate?" said Victor. My father stared at him uncomprehendingly.

"Your car," said Victor again. Eventually, my father motioned vaguely towards the shop entrance, without really thinking what he was doing. As if in a dream, he turned to follow, before the sales assistant brought him up short.

"Sir? You forgot your information pack. There's your complete feed history . . . vaccination and disease eradication certificate . . . comprehensive pedigree . . . corporate history of The Happy Piggery PLC . . . oh, and a complementary jar of apple sauce." He turned to me, and made a patronising attempt at a smile. "Is this for your Feast, young man?" he said. I nodded. He smiled again, "I hope you enjoy it. Don't be frightened of the taste. It's really quite pleasant, once you get used to it."

My father's car was very small, and Flossie was a surprisingly large animal. There was also more than a whiff of the farmyard about her and we had to drive with the windows open and the rain pouring in all the way home to stop ourselves gagging. I spent most of the journey kneeling up in the front passenger's seat trying to restrain her from mauling my father. She kept making horrible squealing noises that made him wince, and several times she lurched violently from one side of the car to the other, forcing him to take rapid corrective action with the steering wheel. The only thing he said to me the entire journey was a blunt request to keep that bloody animal quiet.

When we got home, Flossie nearly broke loose, but we managed to rein her in and drag her into the house, whist my mother stood watching us and tut-tutting from time to time. Manoeuvring a large pig through a small terraced house is not an easy matter, and several ornaments bit the dust on the way. Flossie was also quite wet from the rain, and she left a muddy trail of footprints in the hall, much to my mother's disgust. But in the end, with one last heave, we pushed the pig out through the back door, and she was safely in the yard.

"Well, that's it for now," said my father as he shut the back door again.

"I hope you're not planning to leave it there," said my mother, who was standing in the kitchen opposite him with her arms folded.

"Um . . . well . . . I was rather . . ."

"Oh, come on, you're being ridiculous. You're putting things off again, aren't you? What if it escapes? What if it wants feeding during the night? No, you've got to kill it now. Where's that captive bolt?"

My father shook his head. "We can't use that. You see . . ."

My mother rolled her eyes to the ceiling. "Ye Gods! How much did you pay for those classes? Didn't they teach you anything? How are you going to do it then?"

"I've . . . I've . . . I've got to slit her throat."

My mother looked at my father in disbelief, and then roared with laughter. "You?" she said, "You? Slit that thing's throat? Well, this I have *got* to see!"

My father just shook his head nervously, whilst my mother went to the knife drawer and selected one.

"Here," she said, holding it up to the light, "This is the sharpest. Go on, take it. Take it!"

"I don't think I can . . ." he said, but my mother forestalled him with a look. He shook his head again and then snatched the knife angrily from her. I followed him outside, where we found Flossie mournfully grubbing in the drain by the back door. As soon as she saw the knife in my father's hand, she got wind that something unpleasant was about to happen, and took off squealing towards the back of the yard. My father lunged at her wildly and missed completely. A few faces began to appear at upstairs windows as neighbours realised what was going on.

Slipping and sliding on the wet concrete, we chased her to the back wall, whereupon she changed direction and charged at my father. At least this time he made contact, although the net result was only a deep gash on her flank. She squealed in agony and bolted back towards the house, bleeding profusely and making the most appalling racket. A cheer or two went up from our audience. This was good entertainment.

We had her cornered this time. I covered the left side, whilst my father advanced from the right, knife in hand. Flossie looked at us both with an expression of blind panic. Out of the corner of my eye, I could see my father, looking about as terrified as she was and half-blinded by the rain on his glasses. Then he lurched forward, stabbing vainly at her throat, as she simultaneously made her move back towards him. She knocked the knife clean out of his right hand, causing a slight cut to his left in the process. He yelped, then quickly reached into his pocket to fetch out his handkerchief, which he wrapped round the wound. Meanwhile, Flossie was back down the other end of the yard.

I slowly advanced towards her, looking her straight in the eye, until I was only a metre or so away from her. Then I edged closer, little by little, until I could almost touch her. Once more pace nearer, and I grabbed her round the neck. She wriggled and twisted, squealing furiously, but it was all to no avail; I had her tight.

"Dad!" I said, "Give me the knife!"

He wandered absent-mindedly back towards me, as if he hadn't properly heard.

"Dad! The knife!"

He slowly went back for it, but he seemed reluctant to hand it over. Finally, he shrugged, and gave it to me. I quickly slit the pig's throat in the way that the man from The Happy Piggery had described, and it was all over. A slow, ironic clap started up at one of the upstairs windows. Everyone else closed their curtains and went back to their supper.

I looked up at my father, expecting, I suppose, some kind of "Well done!" or "That's my boy!" But there was nothing. He just stood there motionless in the pouring rain, with blood on his shoes, and I suppose it might have been the rain, but I could have sworn that there were tears in his eyes.

AFTER THE RAPTURE

After the Rapture, tempers frayed in the long queue outside the pearly gates. "Loaves or fishes, anyone?" snickered Lucifer from his van.

NATURAL SELECTION

Hinchcliffe placed his elbows on the desk in front of him and leant forward, peering at me over the top of his glasses.

"So, how have you enjoyed the weekend?" he said.

Nerve-wracking? Ball-breaking? Pant-wetting? Arse-clenching? Scrotum-shredding? Sphincter-ripping?

"It's been great," I eventually settled for. "Challenging," I added.

"Good ... good," he said. His colleague, whom I didn't recognise but had been introduced as Samantha from Human Resources, did likewise. "Well, then," he said, "as you've probably realised by the fact that you're still here, you did pretty well in most of the tests."

"Yeah, thanks," I said. Apart from, of course, the small matter of the blackout during the jungle treasure hunt exercise. But he was right. Overall, I had done very well, both on the physical and intellectual tests. Even the raft-building had turned out to be a success, which was a surprise. Although if I were to be completely honest with myself, it had been more down to that guy Jensen than anything else.

"So now we come to the part where we try to find a little more about what makes you tick, eh?" He evidently wasn't going to give much more away about how I was doing. But, as he said, the fact that I was still here was the most tangible indication that I was still very much in the running. People had been disappearing at regular intervals throughout the whole weekend; the number at each meal break was visibly dwindling. And looking at those who'd been there at lunch today, the choice was likely to end up being between Jensen and myself. The rest were, frankly, a bunch of losers.

"What is it that makes you want to work for Interquor?" said Samantha from HR. At first sight, she looked thirty-ish, although closer inspection put her in her mid-forties. Slight of build, but she clearly knew how to dress to best effect. Tight hair. Tailored suit. Colour Me Beautiful accessories. Probably tough as nails.

Why did I want to work for this bunch? The obvious answer was the advertised salary range. Or, to be more accurate, the top end of it, which was almost double what I was currently on. And that was without the potential bonus being taken into consideration. But, hell, I was worth it.

"I want to develop my skills in a go-ahead organisation with trans-global reach, a firm ethical stance and penetration into a comprehensive portfolio of vertical markets," I said.

Hey, that was good.

She gave me a rather dubious look and glanced at Hinch-cliffe. I couldn't read him at all. I'd seen him a few times during the weekend, but I hadn't managed to get a word with him before today. He was probably in his late thirties, tanned complexion, not a hair out of place, with deep blue eyes that flattered and threatened you by turns.

"But what do you think you can offer us?" he said, and I thought I detected a slight edge underneath the polite tone of voice.

"I . . . well, as you can see, I have several years' experience of marketing in this sector . . ."

"We've read your CV," he said. "Tell us something we don't know."

"Right . . ." I gave them a halting account of how I'd rescued the Actonoid campaign last year. I left out some of the juicier details. Given Interquor's statement on corporate ethics that was prominently displayed on their website, I felt it prudent not to go into some of the more dubious stunts that I'd pulled in order to put our competitors out of the game. Although, frankly, if they'd done their homework properly, they probably knew about everything I'd done – up to and including the incident with the Danish rent boys.

"Interesting," he said. "Tell me what you think about ethics."

Well, that was something of a curveball. I played for time. "Personal or corporate?" I asked.

He narrowed his eyes slightly. "There's a difference?" he said.

Bugger.

"Ha ha, of course not," I said, back-pedalling furiously. "It's very unlikely that the two would ever diverge."

"Hmmm. Interesting. Could you ever imagine a situation where they might?"

"I'm sorry . . . I don't really . . ."

"Well, as an example, what would you do if you were asked to do something that offended your personal set of ethics?"

"That would be difficult."

"Hmmm. Well, let's park that for a moment. How would you define your own personal ethical position?"

"I . . . would . . . say . . . say that everything I do is informed by a moral code."

"And this is something innate?"

"Well, yes."

"Something that is second nature to you?"

"Definitely."

"Hmmm. I see." At this point, he looked at Samantha from HR, eyebrows raised. She nodded. He looked back at me.

"You were in the same raft-building team as a Mr Jensen, I believe?"

"Er, yes."

"Indeed. He was rather good – better than you were, in fact, wasn't he?"

I looked straight back at him. I wasn't going to agree with

that, however true it was. I didn't like the way this was going.

"Then again," he said, "you scored higher than him in some of the other activities. In fact, over the whole weekend, you were pretty much even, and both of you were ahead of the pack by some way. But you realised that, didn't you?"

This time, I did nod. Then he did something curious. He produced a black and white picture and laid it out in front of me. I was glad it was in black and white.

"This is how we found Mr Jensen after the jungle treasure hunt."

Holy Jesus Christ.

Jensen (if indeed it was him) was scarcely recognisable. He had been slashed to ribbons and he was lying in a pool of a dark liquid, which I assumed to be blood. My first thought was one of absolute horror. I am ashamed to say that my second thought was one of elation that I had got the job. But there was more to come.

Hinchcliffe picked up the photograph, stood up and went over to a safe in the wall. He unlocked it and removed a DVD and a plastic bag containing a bloody knife. He tossed the bag down in front of me.

"I wonder if you can explain why your fingerprints are on this?" he said.

I gaped back at him, completely at a loss for words.

"I didn't think so. Disconcerting, isn't it? You'll find this a bit strange as well." He inserted the DVD into the PC on his desk and then flicked a switch. A screen opened up in the wall behind him, and he swivelled around in his chair to watch.

The screen showed a section of the jungle treasure hunt circuit. In the middle of the screen I could see Jensen digging around at the base of a tree. Eventually, he seemed to have found something, because he was holding it in his hands. It looked like an ostrich egg.

"We have cameras all around the set," said Hinchcliffe. "Health and safety."

I could scarcely watch as I saw myself coming into shot.

No, creeping into shot. Christ, I was stalking him. Worse than that, I was carrying a knife. The knife that Hinchcliffe had just shown to me.

"I think what impressed us all was the way in which you'd targeted him," he said, looking to Samantha from HR for confirmation. "You'd realised that he was your main rival, and you just went for him. Very direct."

On the screen, I was edging closer to Jensen. When I was in striking distance, I must have disturbed him, because he suddenly stood up and turned round to face me. The sound was fuzzy so I couldn't hear what I was saying at this point, but I appeared to be shouting and gesticulating with the knife. I seemed to be asking him to give me the egg. But he just held it to his chest. Then the attack started. I looked away, waiting for it to be over.

"It's a nice technique you've got there," said Hinchcliffe, miming a vague slashing movement in the air. "Do you play squash? I'd hate to be up against your backhand." Samantha from HR rolled her eyes and shook her head at him as if admonishing a naughty boy.

I was feeling sick. I glanced up at the screen. Jensen was now on the ground, but I was still hacking away at him. Finally, it was over, and I watched myself bend down to pick up the egg from the ground where Jensen had dropped it. Then I sank to my knees and slowly keeled over, still clutching it.

"Hmmm. Interesting," said Hinchcliffe, as he ejected the DVD and put it back in the wall safe along with the bloody knife. "We don't always see that kind of reaction. You're something quite special."

"I'm . . . sorry?" My voice was quiet. Trembling.

"When you arrived on Friday night, you signed a waiver form. Do you remember that?"

"Well, yes."

"Giving us permission to treat you with any drugs that we saw fit over the course of the recruitment weekend."

"Did I?" I hadn't bothered reading it. It looked like stand-ard health and safety bullshit.

"Yes, you did. Well, there's a drug that we sometimes use to evaluate the level of aggression that a candidate might show in a tight spot."

"There is? How . . . ?" I began.

"Well, we are a pharmaceutical company," he said. "It's what we do." He paused. "Actually, we've been developing it for the military. Seems they have a problem with some of their precious soldiers not wanting to get killed." The edge in his voice that I'd detected earlier was rapidly working its way to centre stage.

"So you . . . drugged . . . me . . ."

"All of you, to be strictly accurate. All of you that were left at that point, anyway. It's an interesting drug. It brings things out. It shows you what someone might just be capable of if they were really pushed. And sometimes we need that at Interquor. Sometimes we need a little more raw aggression and a little less respect for petty rules. We know what you're really like now. So don't give me that crap about ethics ever again."

I looked at each of them in turn. They seemed to be expect-ing me to say something, but I couldn't think of anything.

"Well then," said Hinchcliffe, the edge in his voice now gone. "If you've nothing to say, I think that probably con-cludes the interview." He extended a hand. "Welcome aboard!"

"I'm sorry? Don't I have a choice?"

There was an almost imperceptible jerk of his head towards the wall safe.

"Why wouldn't you want to join us?" he said, with a slight shrug.

"I . . . but that's blackmail!" I said. Hinchcliffe looked offended.

"Ooh, that's a word we try not to use around here," he said. "No, no, no. You wanted this job when you walked in the room, didn't you? Well, we're offering it to you. If that's blackmail" – he made an expansive gesture – "well, bring it on, I say." He leaned closer to me. "Of course, we do like to be sure of absolute loyalty in our new employees. But can you blame us for that?"

I shook my head. He was right. I did want the job. It was just that I didn't want it quite like this. I tried to re-introduce a sense of normality to the proceedings. "Can we discuss salary, then?" I said.

He looked surprised. "Oh, well yes, I suppose we ought to do that." He looked at Samantha from HR, who asked me what kind of figure I was thinking of.

"I guess I was hoping for something near the top of your advertised range," I said. This was apparently a very funny remark.

"I rather think not," she said. "In the present economic climate, that would be out of the question. And besides, don't forget that we know you're a criminal. We have to learn to trust you. You have to show commitment. If you behave yourself, maybe in a few years we might raise you a little. But for the time being, I think it's best if you start at the bottom."

I shook my head. Once again I had no choice. I stood up and turned to go. Then I remembered something that I should have asked earlier.

"What about Jensen?"

"Ah, yes," said Hinchcliffe, smiling. "I was wondering when you'd ask about him. Well, we have a lot of samples of his handwriting – the creative writing part of the weekend is always helpful in these circumstances – and it seems that he's decided on the spur of the moment to abandon this materialistic life and head off around the world. But all sorts of things can happen to a young man in search of adventure, can't they? There are real jungles out there." He paused. "In the meantime, we know exactly where his body's buried. And as you've probably realised, we make it our business to know where all the bodies are buried."

LESS THAN DEADLY

His attempt to commit all seven deadly sins in one week ended in failure. On reflection, it was probably a bad idea to start with sloth.

POSSIBLE SIDE EFFECTS

Oh my God. How did it get to this? I have at least found the tablets, and maybe they will fix everything. Six left. What was it about six? It must take six to fix everything, that must be what it was.

I'll pour myself a shot first, though. I feel like I haven't had a drink for a week, although you wouldn't think so from the state of the place. The furniture has been smashed to pieces, there are books and CDs scattered all over the floor and there are burn marks on the carpet.

There is also a body in the hall. It's a young woman. She's pretty, in an unsophisticated sort of way, and if all things were equal, I might fancy her. She'd probably be my type, if I had such a thing as a type. But, as I said, there's no point in fancying her, because she is, after all, dead. Slashed to pieces.

I have no idea how she came to be in my hallway. All I can assume is that someone dragged her in there to keep her out of harm's way until such time as they could come back and bury her. I would imagine that kind of thing goes on all the time around here. Although I'm not really sure of anything these days.

Six tablets to make everything right, washed down with finest Stolichnaya. Here goes.

Yesterday

Dark. Oh God, it's dark.

Two Days Ago

Don't know how many tablets left. Lost the tablets. Lost the fucking tablets. Fuckfuckfuckfuckfuckfuck. How can I lose the fucking tablets?

So much pain.

Dark.

Everything is dark.

I am being besieged. The bastards are trying to invade my territory. Why do they hate me? They stuff things through my letterbox. Paper with writing on it. Words that make no sense. I can't read any more. My eyes hurt too much.

One of them has managed to get through the door. Christ! They have sent a woman to torment me. She must have stolen a key from somewhere. Starts off by shouting at me and then she tries to grab hold of me.

Luckily I have my knife with me.

She has let go of me, but she is all red now. I hate red.

Three Days Ago

Nine tablets left. This morning I climbed naked onto the roof to watch the sunrise. I have given up wearing clothes. Clothes are false. I need truth. I am the truth. I am the way, the truth and, oh yes, I am the fucking life as well. Worship me, for I am holy.

Someone called Jemma keeps phoning me. I know of no one called Jemma. She sounds false. When I tell her she sounds false, she cries. I listen to her weeping. It is an unearthly, tinkly sound. Perhaps I could like her if she wasn't false. But there is no room in the world for falsity.

And why weep anyway? In a truthful world, there is no need for tears. Tears are a sign of falsehood.

Four Days Ago

Twelve tablets left. Bliss was it that dawn to be alive! Wow! I am transformed! This is fantastic. Unbelievable. I am cured. Repeat that after me. I. Am. Cured. My body is a temple. It is sacred.

Went for a walk today on the common. The sun will shine for evermore. Everybody is beautiful. I danced with a lollipop lady across her zebra crossing. I am the zebra. I am black. I am white. I am all the colours of the rainbow.

I don't even care that Jemma has gone. I don't need her now. I am self-sufficient. Love me, and I will love you. Hate me and I will love you anyway. I am love. We are all love.

Five Days Ago

Fourteen tablets left. I'm feeling a little better! Well, I think I am. The pain is beginning to subside, and I can bend down to pick things up now. It's odd: I feel stronger than I did before. Maybe that's how it works. I've also got a strange kind of contented feeling, as if I'm at peace with the world.

What's really weird is that several times today, I'm been convinced that I've been hearing music. Nothing recognisable, not a tune as such. Something deeper than that. Something primeval: the music of the spheres. I can almost feel my body vibrating in time with it. It's as if I am tuned in to the cosmos. I can feel the breath of the stars.

Jemma's not speaking to me this evening. Claims I slapped her when she complained about me not doing the washing up. As if I'd do that. Well fuck her.

Six Days Ago

I have fifteen tablets left. Enough for just over two weeks. Dr Burton says that I should be feeling better after a few days, but that I must continue to the end of the course to stop it recurring. The pills are small and white. How can something as small and insignificant as that fix something as big as my pain?

They taste of nothing. How do I know they're not just a placebo?

Had a row with Jemma this evening. Can't remember what it was about. Sometimes it's hard to get through to her. She's a lovely girl, but she can be a bit dim.

One Week Ago

Got an emergency appointment, with new lady doctor. Nice legs. For a moment I'm distracted enough to wonder about shifting the discussion to maybe some kind of imaginary problem with the old waterworks. But the next spasm shifts all that out of my head. Christ, it's awful.

Dr Burton isn't helpful at first. Not a lot they can do about chronic pain apparently. Maybe try acupuncture (bollocks) or herbal medicine (even more bollocks). So bollocks is all there is on offer then. Then she says have I considered Gramapraxyl. I've heard that name before somewhere. Some kind of miracle cure. Sounds like more bollocks to me, but at least it's bollocks with a bit of science behind it, and the way I feel right now I'll try anything. And I have decided I trust Dr Burton. She's lovely.

Dr Burton tells me not to look it up on the internet, because there's a lot of crap been published about it. Possible side effects, that kind of thing. But every drug has them. Just be careful not to exceed the stated dose. One per day. More than that can seriously fuck with your head, and half a dozen is fatal. And never mix with alcohol. So I've got to remember not to count to more than one, and stay dry for the next couple of weeks. Shouldn't be too hard.

As I leave the surgery, I realise where I've heard of Gramapraxyl. Every bloody freebie in there has got it on, from the clock to her reflex hammer. Oh, sod it. Too much pain to worry about the niceties.

Jemma seems happy now that I've gone to the doctor's. She cooked my favourite stroganoff for me tonight. At times like this I can't believe how lucky I am.

Ten Days Ago

The pain is unbelievable. I can't concentrate, I can't work and I can't sleep. I cannot function as a human being. Jemma keeps nagging me, saying that I should go to the doctor but, frankly, they're all a bunch of complete charlatans in the pay of the fucking pharmaceutical conglomerates. I can't stand doctors. I think Jemma fancies Dr Harrison. God knows, he's already had his hand up most of her intimate orifices, so he's got a head start if he's remotely interested. And quite frankly, the way I feel right now, he can have her, the unsympathetic cow.

I've had this pain for, what, three weeks is it now? I bent down to reach something underneath my desk, felt a click and as soon as I stood up again, my whole body was screaming at me, and it hasn't stopped since. Jemma says I don't get enough exercise, the bitch. Jemma says that I'm too fat. Jemma says that it's no wonder that my spine's giving out with all the excess weight it's got to carry.

Right now I don't give a toss what Jemma thinks. All I want to do is crawl into a corner and die.

MISUNDERSTANDINGS

On our first date, she said she was an animal lover, which sounded promising until I realised that "animal" was not an adjective. However, at least I now knew how to win her heart.

So I bought a small white mouse for her, called Benji. After a week with him, I became quite attached and I felt unbearably sad at the prospect of giving him away.

On our second date, I presented the gift to her as she opened the door to her flat. She hesitated briefly. Then, smiling, she took Benji from me and fed him to her python.

MR NATHWANI'S HAIKU

He used to write a lot of poetry, but that was a long time ago. He would write soppy love poems to Lakshmi when they were courting. She would scold him for it and make fun of him, but secretly she was flattered. It was an arranged marriage, of course, but that didn't necessarily preclude them falling in love. Their life together stretched out in front of them like the twin tracks of the East African Railway that their fathers had crossed the ocean to build.

He wrote his last poem in gaol. It was a vessel for his anger, to stop him doing something stupid, and it kept him alive during those desperate few months. He never found out what he had done wrong, because they never charged him with anything, but he suspected that it had something to do with being Asian and owning the most successful car dealership in Kampala. In the event, he was released just as arbitrarily as he had been imprisoned. But he didn't have a chance to get back to any semblance of normality, because within a few weeks the order had gone out that all Asians were to be expelled from the country.

England was cold and wet, and Lakshmi suffered terribly from morning sickness. They lived with her relatives in Southall until they could find a place of their own. With what little money that they had managed to bring out with them, they put down a deposit on a small corner shop. The man who sold it to them seemed relieved to have it taken off his hands, even if it was to one of "your lot". Mr Nathwani said nothing. He was learning that to say nothing was often the right thing to do.

Selling groceries was not really like selling cars, but they had no choice. They hardly ever left the shop, except to stock up at the cash and carry. All they did was work and sleep. Lakshmi was stacking shelves in her final month. At night, she dreamt of walking through a landscape populated by cheetahs and antelopes, underneath wide African skies that went on forever. Mr Nathwani dreamt of slop buckets and muffled screams.

As soon as Suresh could count, he helped work the till. He was a bright lad, and his parents were determined to give him the best education that they could afford. When he grew older, he would complain that they never went anywhere, and he would ask his father why he was always working in the shop. Mr Nathwani would reply that he was doing this so that Suresh wouldn't have to.

Lakshmi never really settled in England. Mr Nathwani had promised her that one day he'd take her back, but somehow the shop had become his whole life. She hated the shop, and eventually she left him to it. And when Suresh had left for university, she had nothing at all to do, except watch scratchy VHS tapes of Bollywood films all day long, mouthing silently along to Asha Bhosle. The death certificate might have said cancer, but Mr Nathwani knew that she had died of a broken heart, and he realised bitterly that he had failed her.

She wasn't there to back her husband up when Suresh refused to have an arranged marriage. Mr Nathwani was furious, partly on principle and partly because there was something about Rushma that he didn't care for. Too modern, although – as Suresh was quick to point out – at least she was a bloody Hindu. They were only just back on speaking terms when baby Quentin was born five months later. He felt that it might have been more appropriate at least to name the child after an Indian film director rather than some damn

American, but he managed to keep his mouth shut.

Mr Nathwani liked being a grandfather, although he wasn't able to spend as much time with his grandson as he would have liked, because of the shop. Suresh kept trying to persuade him to sell up, but he held out for several years more, until the stroke. Whilst his father was recovering, Suresh negotiated a deal with a major chain that would secure him a comfortable retirement. But for all the pride that Mr Nathwani felt at his son's skill in drawing up such a clever contract, he felt a profound sense of emptiness after he had signed it.

He lived in a large comfortable flat, not far away from Suresh and Rushma, but he didn't visit them very often. They inhabited a strange world. He had never understood how anyone could allow themselves to live on credit, and he was baffled by the number of cards that they seemed to flash around. On the other hand, he understood a lot about cars, but he still couldn't fathom why Suresh needed to upgrade to a smarter model every couple of years. And why did Rushma need all those pairs of shoes? They didn't seem to make her any happier.

They lived in a big house surrounded by high gates and surveillance cameras. Well, that was nothing new. Everywhere you went these days, you were watched by these cameras. Mr Nathwani wasn't at all sure about this. Granted, the cameras might have caught the little toe-rags that tried to firebomb the shop back in the eighties – and he still thanked whichever God it was that had reminded him to put a bucket of water underneath the letterbox before he went to bed that night. But it also occurred to him that some people back in the old country in the seventies would also have loved to have had access to that kind of technology.

Mr Nathwani hardly saw his son at all. Suresh worked long hours in the City, and always seemed exhausted when he was at home. Quentin was a complete stranger to his grandfather. When they were in the same room, Mr Nathwani would try to engage him in conversation about what he'd done at school, and he would receive grunts by way of reply. But most of the time, the boy hid away in his bedroom. Whenever Mr Nathwani asked Rushma what he did up there, she would shrug and say either "TV" or "internet".

Time drifted on. But Mr Nathwani had all the time in the world.

Dr Hussain was a tiny slip of a thing. A Muslim, of course, but she talked more sense than the other idiots at the practice. She explained that depression was very common in people of his age. She could prescribe him tablets, which he would probably have to take for the rest of his life, but she didn't feel that he was really the type who wanted to be locked into that. Or – and here she paused, as if she wasn't sure if she should really be suggesting this – he could try these people. She handed him a card, saying apologetically that they were nominally a Christian organisation. Mr Nathwani replied that no one was perfect, and they both laughed.

At the retreat house, Mr Nathwani lived in a room with walls that were bare save for a figurine spread out on a cross. He studied it closely on arrival, shaking his head. He never had really got his head around what a truly bizarre religion Christianity was. His faith was so much more practical. But the brothers were friendly and open, and after a couple of weeks he felt sufficiently at ease with them to start talking about his life. He even mentioned the poetry.

A day or so after this, one of the brothers came to see him, and asked if he had ever tried writing a haiku. Sometimes working in such a restricted form could be liberating, the brother explained. Mr Nathwani smiled, and said that he couldn't possibly manage to do that. The brother simply put a pad of paper and a pencil on the table next to the bed and left without saying another word.

After an hour or so, Mr Nathwani looked at what he had written:

All live in cages
The best that we can hope for
Is to choose our own

Well, it was a start.

THE EXPERIMENT

Professor the said, "surprise a was that, well." Backwards run to began time, on machine the switched they when.

ANNIVERSARY FEAST

Jake filled up the glasses from the still and set them down on the console. Strictly speaking, this was breaking enough of the company's rules to earn him instant dismissal. But there wasn't anyone in a position to do that within several parsecs, so he reckoned he was probably safe. And besides, this was a special occasion.

"Here's to another ten years, eh?" he said, taking a slug from his glass. Whew. This was powerful stuff.

"And then two more to landfall," said Gary, downing his in one go before handing his glass out for a refill. "Some trip. Y'know, sometimes I wish I was one of those bastards snoozing away in the hold."

"You're kidding?"

Gary laughed. "Yeah, I'm kidding. Wouldn't want anyone pissing about with me when I was asleep."

Jake smiled. It was true. You got bored on a trip like this. Let's face it, being an Ark Pilot wasn't exactly a demanding job. The only qualification you needed was to be so pathologically in debt that the only way to save your family was to take a one-way trip into deep space.

But, man, was it dull.

The face painting had got out of hand. When you've got a hold full of colonists in suspended animation, it's just so tempting to take a magic marker and draw the odd moustache on a face or two. But if there are two of you, it gets competitive. And it wasn't long before the entire hold got to look like a practice session for a Kabuki make-up class. That was going to take some cleaning up before they got to their destination.

And if the truth were told, they'd both fooled around with some of the women as well. Just a bit of a fondle, nothing more. Although Jake wondered about Gary sometimes. He had an odd look to him sometimes when he came back from the hold.

"So what's for supper?" said Jake. It was Gary's turn to be in charge of the catering.

Gary looked thoughtful. "I fancy something a bit different. Not the usual freeze-dried shit. I think we deserve something real tonight. Some proper meat."

Jake raised an eyebrow. "Like where are we going to get hold of that, man? Pardon me for being a bit thick, but I don't recall passing a flock of interstellar sheep lately."

Gary smiled. Jake knew that smile. It meant that Gary had had one of his ideas.

"Remember that fire in bay 12?" said Gary.

"So?"

"Remember the smell? The burning flesh? Bit like pork?"

Jake stared at Gary.

"I like pork," said Gary.

"Well, I'm not allowed to eat it," said Jake.

"Bet your rabbi didn't mention what I'm thinking of," said Gary. "And are you going to fill up my glass or not?"

"Well, what d'you think?" said Gary, picking his teeth.

"What do I think?" said Jake. "Well, I'm just wondering how many of those fuckers they'll miss. I mean, how many people d'you really need to build a colony?"

PERFECT MOMENT

"I want this perfect moment to last forever," she'd said. But after a century together in the time bubble, he was beginning to annoy her.

HOW I BECAME A
NEW MAN AND WHAT
GOOD IT DID ME

If I say that it all started when I was having my nails done, I can see you're going to get the wrong idea, so let me state right from the start that I am a rampant, red-blooded straight-down-the-middle fully heterosexual male. I present as evidence for this my lust for Madeleine from Emerging Markets, the thought of whose perfect form filled my every waking hour and rather too many of my night-time ones. Moreover, this new-found interest in personal grooming on my part was entirely for Madeleine's sake.

How can I describe Madeleine? There were so many things. The way her long black hair fell over her eyes when she tilted her head just so. The delicate way she brushed it away with her hand. Her slender wrists. The nape of her neck. Her firm yet slim thighs. Her pert —

"OK, love, can we move on to the right hand now?" The voice of the beautician rudely broke into my daydream. It was so easy to drift off when your eyes were covered up with a couple of pieces of cucumber.

"So who's this Madeleine, then?" she said.

"I beg your pardon?"

"Madeleine. You was mumbling about her." She giggled.

"You was in a little world of your own, there."

I smiled ruefully. "She's a girl . . . at work . . . I—"

"Asked her out yet?"

"Good lord, no. I—"

I could almost hear her rolling her eyes. "Oh dear," she said. "Oh dear, oh dear. Let me guess. You wanted to wait until you'd tarted yourself up a bit. Well, let me tell you, sunshine, it's going to take more than a manicure and a facial to turn you into Mr Love Pants."

"I beg your pardon? Hey, I didn't come here to be—"

"Calm down, lover boy. I'm about to offer you the best advice you've heard in your life."

"I'm sorry?"

"What you need is our comprehensive holistic personal renovation treatment. Make you a new man. 'Course it ain't cheap, but I'd guess that a geeky bugger like you makes a decent wedge."

"So what does that involve?" I said. I was intrigued.

"I'll get you a brochure when we're done. Fifteen per cent discount if you sign up today. Now spread your fingers, OK?"

So it was that I signed up for a week-long holistic personal renovation course at a health spa in the country. I say "health spa", although in reality, Camp X-Ray with Pilates and mung beans was closer to the mark. But by now I was ready to suffer anything to get my hands on Madeleine. Since my visit to the beauty salon, she had turned up at my desk out of the blue, asking me for a report on Moldova. Unfortunately, I was too busy trying to remember where the fuck Moldova was to come up with a slick response, so our first contact could not be considered a great success.

But she spoke to me. Her voice was like the chattering of a thousand love-birds. And she came close enough for me to smell her. She smelt of innocence. Of purity. Of perfection.

Oh God.

"You've gone off again, haven't you?" said the elocution teacher. "What was I saying?"

"Something about the rain in Spain?" I said. From his frosty response, I could tell that I was more than a little wide of the mark.

The elocution classes were tiresome, but at least they were more pleasant than the strenuous exercise programme that I was subjected to. Each day started with a ten-mile run around the perimeter of the complex. This was followed up by an exhausting circuit around the weights equipment supervised by a monosyllabic muscle-bound hulk called Sven. I grew to hate Sven, almost as much as I hated Roger from Export Credit Control. Ah yes, Roger.

Roger had had his eye on Madeleine for as long as I had. He fancied himself as a ladies' man. He was a balding little git with a slick moustache and a line in cheesy jokes that no one in the office found remotely amusing. Frankly, there was no way that he stood a chance with her – she was way too classy for a slug like him – but I found it galling to see how he was managing to smarm his way into working with her at every opportunity.

"Lat pull-down. Twenty reps," said Sven, nudging me none too lightly in the small of the back.

I will pass over the other weirdos that I had to deal with in that place. There was the nutritionist, who spent half an hour poking around in my stools with a stick, all the time fixing me with a beady, disapproving eye. And there was the assertiveness coach, who spent our session devising a convoluted rôle-play in which I had to explain to him how unhappy I was that he had buggered my mother, whilst all the time maintaining the correct body language and a reasonable, non-aggressive and appropriate tone of voice.

But the most humiliating part of the week was the appointment with the plastic surgeon. The first thing he said when I closed the door behind me was, "OK, get your kit off and stand over there." I did the usual "Who, me?" thing, before realising that he was indeed looking in my direction. Once I had disrobed and was standing shivering in the middle of the room, he began to walk slowly around me, making odd marks on my body from time to time with a felt-tip pen.

"Streuth! Well, we've got some work to do, here, haven't we?" he said, examining me with evident distaste. "From what the other guys have been telling me about your ambitions, I was expecting Brad Fucking Pitt to walk in the room." He paused, as if trying to make a difficult decision. "How soon d'you want to make your move?"

"As soon as I get back to work, of course," I said. Before Dodgy Roger gets his teeth into her, I thought.

"And you want to stride into her office like a God?"

"Well, yes," I said.

"In which case, the choice you have is between Zeus" – here he prodded me in the stomach – "or Buddha."

Which wasn't much of a choice, frankly.

"So I guess we're looking at a bit of the old lipo," he said.

"Sorry?"

"Liposuction. Suck out all that unnecessary gunk, and I can get you looking like an Adonis by Sunday tea-time." He paused for a moment. "And whilst we're at it, how's your old fellah down there?"

"My what?"

"Your love shovel. Your shag spike. Your todger."

"What do you mean?"

"Well, does it do the business? It's no good getting the cylinder oiled if the old piston doesn't touch the sides, is it?" He picked up a magnifying glass from his desk. "And if you ask me, you've been a bit short-changed in that department, mate."

"It's a bit cold in here," was all I could manage by way of reply.

When I returned home, I was a new man. Confident, healthy, slim, fit and with an air of supreme confidence – to say nothing of a little bit extra in the trouser department. I was ready for Madeleine. But first I had to finish that Moldova report. I put my heart and soul into it – twenty hours a day for a whole week, until at four o'clock on Friday it was ready for delivery. It was a masterpiece.

I stood outside Madeleine's office, trying to remember everything that I'd been told. I was about to knock, when I heard laughter coming from inside. I almost turned around and walked away when I remembered that I was a new man now. So I rapped smartly on the door and went straight in without waiting for a reply.

There was a flurry of activity as the two people in the room adjusted their clothing. The one I recognised was Roger from Export Credit Control, standing behind the desk, smirking at me. He was still the same old balding mustachioed tosser. But the blonde woman sitting at the desk, buttoning an ill-fitting blouse over her vast, surgically enhanced cleavage, was completely unknown to me. At first. Then, as she looked up at me, I realised with horror that it was Madeleine. I gaped at her, unable to speak.

"Can I help you?" she said. A waft of cheap scent hit me full in the face. And what had she had done to her lips? Collagen?

"Er . . . report on Moldova. Like you asked. Y'know," I said.

"Ah, it's you," she said. "You look different."

"S-so do you," I countered.

She sniggered, looking down at her enormous bosom. "So I do, don't I? It was Roger's idea," she said, looking up at him. "Wasn't it, tiger?" Roger responded with a ridiculous "Rrarrr" noise.

I couldn't take any more of this. I flounced out of the office, slamming the door behind me. As I walked back to my desk, I realised that in doing so, I'd damaged one of my nails. Sometimes it's the little details that hurt the most.

LOVE STORY, DAY ONE

It started with sidelong glances at the meat counter. I bought sausages; she bought liver. "Fancy a mixed grill?" I said.

THE GUITARIST'S
INHERITANCE

I'm a perfectionist. I've inherited that from my mother, although I wonder sometimes if it's more something that we've both acquired through circumstance. Even though I've long since left home, she still comes to all my gigs, and she watches me like a hawk, trying to detect any flaws in my playing. She tries to be inconspicuous, but I can always see her in the audience. I'd know those eyes anywhere; I've got a pair just like them. Sometimes she comes backstage, hanging back shyly as if she can't believe that I'm there. Sometimes she just disappears into the night, calling me later to give her report.

What about my father? What have I inherited from him? Well, I certainly didn't inherit any cash from him – he was an old-school hippy, hopelessly feckless with money, whether it was his own or other people's. No, it's from him that I got the music: the singing and the guitar playing.

I grew up to the sound of my father playing old Woody Guthrie songs: "This Land is Your Land", "Tom Joad" and the rest. I sometimes include one or two of them in my set, but it's not easy. More than once I've cracked up on stage at the thought of him. Sometimes an inheritance can be a burden.

I have a pretty low-key career. I make just enough to get by, but that's about it. The best thing I can say about my reviewers is that sometimes they are kind. They know who I am, and who my father was, and sometimes I wonder if all they're looking for is a good story. The music is, frankly, secondary. It's more the genetics that they're interested in. Just how like my father am I?

In his day, he was – they say – a pretty mean guitarist, and he could pick a tune with the best. But by the time I was old enough to have any level of discernment, he had lost most of his skill and he would struggle to string a few chords together. It was my mother who taught me most of what I know. She isn't much of a musician, but she's a good teacher. And, like I said, she's a perfectionist.

The one thing that I would love to do would be to play one of his guitars on stage. But that's out of the question. One by one, he smashed them all in an impotent rage, and all I have left are the bent remains of a National Steel that defied his frustrated efforts to destroy it.

On my eighteenth birthday, five years after his death, I found out why my father had such an affinity with Woody Guthrie, although I'd half-guessed the truth already. We'd been studying genetics in biology, and our textbook used the transmission of Huntington's disease as an example of the way that a dominant gene works. I was sure that I'd heard the name before, but I failed to make any connection. If you're that young when a parent dies, you don't ask the obvious questions.

Sometimes when I'm having trouble getting to sleep, I think of the film of Woodstock, and Arlo Guthrie, Woody's son – young, confident and charismatic – singing "Alice's Restaurant". I wonder how he gets through the day, knowing that the odds are 50/50. Just like they are for me.

My mother still comes to all my gigs, and she watches me like a hawk, trying to detect any flaws in my playing. I know why she does this. Like me, she is looking for the first signs. The first fumbled chord. The first slight shake in my plectrum hand. The first early warning of my inheritance.

LOVE STORY, WEEK ONE

It was the way we completed . . . each other's . . . sentences.
It was the way we completed . . . each other.

SO WHAT ARE YOU UP TO THESE DAYS?

They have these reunions every ten years, but I've never been to one before, so it's interesting to see who's changed (the ones who were always youthful-looking) and who hasn't (the ones who have looked middle-aged all their life), and in any case it's a good time to catch up with people you haven't seen since you left the place, if only to see if you're doing better or worse than them. Anyway there's this guy sitting next to me whom I vaguely remember, but I can't quite put a name to: prosperous-looking, tanned, bit of a paunch, obviously doing pretty well for himself. So we do the usual mutual introduction thing, and I remember him now, although I'm struggling to fill in all the details, because (as I say) it's been a while since we last saw each other, and I can't even remember which subject he was reading. He's evasive when I ask him what he's doing these days, but after a few glasses he opens up a bit and tells me that's he's actually in the torture business, which comes as something of a surprise, but these are strange times that we are living in so I try to act as if this is nothing unusual, and start asking him questions like "what's the best thing about being a torturer?" (all the foreign travel apparently), "what's the worst thing about being a torturer?" (again, all the foreign travel) and "how do your kids feel about this?" (no problem, apparently, and they certainly don't get hassled in the playground any more). Then I remember: this guy used to be an activist, a hard-line leftie, a real firebrand, so I mention this to him, pointing out the obvious irony, and he laughs and says to me that he just grew up a little and by the way am I still the same apathetic wishy-washy liberal that I always was? And I say, maybe I am, maybe I'm not, maybe I might be, I'm not sure of anything these days, and he just nods and smiles at me while I blabber away about my insecurities, and I'm quite impressed later on when I realise precisely how much I have given away about myself without even having been shown the instruments.

LOVE STORY, MONTH ONE

"Do you love me?" I said. "Love means never needing to say I love you," she said. "Yes, but do you love me?" I said.

FISHERMEN'S TALES

After circling the island a couple of times, it becomes clear to Milo that there is nowhere that he can safely put ashore, so he drops anchor a little way out. The little rock (for that is all the island really is) seems completely uninhabited, but Milo knows better. There have been too many sightings in the last few weeks, and they can't all be dismissed as the fantasies of lonely fishermen. It's too dark to swim over there now, so he's going to have to wait until first light tomorrow. Milo doesn't mind. He's waited long enough for this, and another night won't kill him.

He radios Steve to give him his end of day report.

"Oh, it's you," says Steve.

"Who else would it be? What's wrong? You still sore you're going to miss out on all the fun?"

"You know that's not it. I just don't think you should be back out there quite yet. It's only been a couple of weeks since . . . well, you know."

"Yeah, I know. I know." He pauses for a moment. "But you've got to understand. It's like one of those getting back into the saddle when you've fallen off things. You know what I mean."

"Milo, you nearly died. Have you forgotten that?"

"Ah, you're exaggerating."

"You know I'm not," says Steve. "Check the repair work on the side of the boat if you need reminding."

Milo is silent for several seconds. "I still say you're jealous," he says.

"Oh, it's no use, is it? What's the weather like out there, anyway? The reports look OK from where I'm sitting."

"Calm as a millpond," says Milo.

"What can you see?"

"Nothing."

"Are you sure you're in the right place?"

"Absolutely. I've triangulated it from all the most reliable reports, and there's nowhere else that it could be. This is definitely it."

"I guess that's it then," says Steve. "So tomorrow you might finally meet one. Well, if you do, give her a kiss for me."

"So you are jealous," says Milo. "Good to see your priorities are still all in working order. As if I would anyway. You know what they say."

"You believe that? Can't say it would stop me."

"In that case, let's wait until I've brought her back, and you can take your chances."

"Now you've got me all excited."

"Oh, control yourself, man. Anyway, I have a tasty vacuum-packed bag of prawn curry that's awaiting my attention, so I'll sign off for the night."

"OK, cheers. Sleep tight." He pauses. "Be careful, mate."

"Yeah, 'course."

Milo flips the switch and the radio goes dead. He's alone on the ocean now: the only human for miles around. He feels calm, relaxed. There's no need to hurry.

Three o'clock in the morning, and the wind is picking up. Water is splashing at the sides of the little boat and there is a gentle to-and-fro rocking motion. Over the sound of the wind, Milo swears he can hear laughter. He gets up from his bunk and goes up on deck. The moonlight is dancing on the waves, and he catches a glimpse of something on the surface. But before he can shine the spotlight on it, it dives down out of sight.

He waits for a while, holding his breath, but nothing else appears. Whatever it is, it knows that he's there and it's not taking any chances. Milo goes back to bed, but it takes an age to get back to sleep and when he does he is plagued by scaly nightmares.

When he awakes with a sore head the next morning, the boat is tossing backwards and forwards in a wild frenzy, and the weather is blowing a gale outside. This didn't show up on the forecast last night. Milo could easily lose his anchor if he doesn't haul it up quickly, so his first priority is to cast the boat loose. Next he needs to get the engine started so that he can at least maintain his position. Once he's done that, Milo takes stock of the situation. Clearly a swim to the island is now out of the question, and if the weather gets any worse, he's going to have to make a break for it back to the mainland. But he can't go back empty-handed. He's come too far for that.

So Milo opts for Plan B. He didn't want to do this, but he has no choice. He opens the fridge and takes out the bait. He prepares a couple of lines, baits the hooks and casts them out into the sea behind the boat. It's not easy work trying to do this in a storm, struggling to maintain his footing on the roller-coaster deck, but after a lot of sliding around Milo manages to set everything up as he wants. Then he starts moving the boat in a gentle arc, trailing the lines behind it. With any luck, maybe the one that was circling him last night will fall for the bait.

Sure enough, after about half an hour of this, something takes hold of the line. Immediately, he stops the boat, and begins to haul in his catch, hoping against hope that he hasn't snagged a dolphin or something. But he's in luck. He's got one. She's flailing around at the end of the line, trying to escape. It's no use, though, and Milo manages to grab hold of her and drag her on board. As soon as he does this, the sea becomes calm again. He's heard it said that they can conjure up a storm from nowhere, but he hasn't believed it until now.

She's wriggling about like a wild thing, and it's all Milo can do to reach inside her mouth and ease the hook out. He does it as gently as he possibly can, but it's still a messy business. As soon as it's free, she coughs twice and spits blood onto his shoes. He offers her a glass of water and she snatches it from him. She drinks it down in one gulp, and hands it back to him with a furious look.

"I'm sorry," he says. "I didn't mean to hurt you. I'm Milo."

She says nothing, but continues to glare at him. He wasn't sure if she would understand him anyway. Some of them were taught English by missionaries in the early part of the last century, but they are few and far between, and this one looks like a wild one.

Milo stands back and appraises her. She measures around five foot from the top of her head to the end of her tail. Long blonde hair, perfect breasts, slightly oily skin, with the classic onset of scales at around her midriff. SeaWorld will pay well for a specimen like this. They could be looking at, what, $100K if he gets her back in one piece.

It's getting hot on deck, now, and she's beginning to dry out. He needs to get her down to the holding tank, so he picks her up in her arms. As Milo catches sight of her face, her expression seems to soften. She puts her arm round his neck, and he feels an unutterable tenderness flow over him. It's impossible to stop himself, despite all the old seamen's admonitions.

He leans in slowly to kiss her. As their lips touch, the world flips through one hundred and eighty degrees, and he feels something pass between them. Something metallic. The hook shoots through Milo's mouth and embeds itself in the back of his throat. Then there's a sudden tug on it and he's pulled off the boat into the water. Inch by inch, the line drags him through the surf towards the rock.

Sitting on top, reeling him in, is a familiar scaly figure.

LOVE STORY, YEAR ONE

When I called to collect my things, my Boba Fett figurine had been smashed into several pieces. "You can glue it together or something, can't you?" she said.

HIDDEN SHALLOWS

Sara puts down her paper and swings her legs over the side of the lounger. Squinting against the lunchtime sun, she peers out over the lake. It looks calm, deep and serene.

"So, fancy a dip, then?" she says.

"Certainly not," says Michaela, not looking up. "Too bloody cold. And besides, we haven't got time. We're due back in half an hour for the afternoon session."

"It's only Smithies," says Sara. "It's been several centuries since he came up with anything remotely new or interesting. Apart from a more lethal form of body odour every other year."

"There's a break-out session on meta-trends in post-feminist rap at the same time, you know."

"Who's leading it?"

"Some German," says Michaela.

"Well, I can take it or leave it." Sara pauses. "I think I'll leave it." She catches sight of something on the surface of the lake, and sits up. "Gosh. He looks cold," she says.

"Who?"

"There's someone swimming out there. Heading in our direction. I'm impressed."

Michaela stirs herself, turns over and pulls herself into a sitting position. "See what you mean," she says. "Bit of a hunk, I'd say."

"Really, Professor, I'm surprised at you." The figure, sporting an impressive six-pack and tiny Speedos, is climbing out of the lake and up onto the sun deck. "Then again," says Sara, "you could be right, my dear."

The two women watch as the young man towels himself down with an extravagant action, before lying, face down, on a lounger some twenty feet away from them.

"Of course, he wouldn't exactly have much in the way of conversation," whispers Michaela.

"I thought you spoke German and Italian pretty well. Covers most of the bases, surely."

"I mean that he's probably thick as two planks dipped in treacle, dimmo. Breakfast could be a little dull."

"And your problem is? I mean, did you see—"

"I did—"

"I mean . . . the—"

"—yes, the size—"

"—the size—"

"—the size of that thing!" they both hiss simultaneously, before collapsing in fits of giggles like a pair of schoolgirls. They are silent for a moment. Sara breaks the silence. "Michaela?"

"Yes?"

"Have you and Gerry ever . . . you know . . . I mean . . . you know . . . what's the most times you've ever done it in one night?"

"Recently?"

"No, ever."

"Well, he managed a couple of times once when we were first going out, but he was so knackered afterwards I didn't have the heart to ask him to try again."

"Yeah. I know the feeling." Sara pauses. "Do you ever wonder what it would be like to have someone like boy wonder over there? I mean, do you ever think we might have it the wrong way around? Could it be more important after all to have one's physical needs met rather than one's intellectual ones?"

"Is that a philosophical question?" says Michaela. "Because if so, you're a bit late to get it onto the programme. Might be worth considering for next year, mind. You could use it to mount an interesting attack on Maslow's bloody hierarchy of needs."

Sara laughs. "No, I was more wondering about our immediate situation."

Michaela looks shocked. "You're kidding. You're not serious, are you?"

"Might be," says Sara, with a little smile. "Call it research." She takes a business card from her bag and starts to scribble a note on the back.

"Hey, show me," says Michaela, making a grab for the card.

"No," says Sara. "Shan't!"

But Michaela's too quick for her. She reads out loud:

soles occidere et redire possunt:
nobis cum semel occidit brevis lux,
nox et perpetua una dormienda.

She nods. "Hmm, Catullus, eh? Well, at least it's not one of the filthy ones."

Sara snatches the card back and gets up. She sneaks over to where the young man is lying. Bending down, she delicately tucks the card into the top of his trunks and steps back. He doesn't move. Sara walks calmly back to her lounger, picks up her belongings and motions to Michaela to go in. Michaela follows her without a word, wide-eyed.

Next morning, over breakfast, Sara looks thoughtful.

"Well?" says Michaela. "Come on, tell me everything. Did he call?"

"Yeah," says Sara. "He called. He called all right. Told me about the mistake—"

"—in the third line? But you knew that, surely?"

"Of course. *Et* instead of *est*. That's why I put it in there.

And that's why I'm upset." She pauses for a moment. "Turns out he's not as dumb as I thought."

"So?"

"So I told him to piss off."

Michaela gives a sympathetic smile. "Life's a bugger sometimes, isn't it?" she says.

"It certainly is," says Sara.

OPPOSITES

She was beautiful, sexy, made of antimatter. Best bang of my life.

ADVICE RE ELEPHANTS

There was no mistaking it. It was definitely an elephant and it was sitting in our living room. The wreckage of several treasured ornaments lay scattered on the floor around it.

"African or Indian?" she called down.

"Dunno," I said. "How do you tell?"

"Size of the ears," she said. "Big ears, African, small ears, Indian."

"You sure?"

"Positive."

I looked at the ears. They seemed quite big to my untutored eye. But I wasn't entirely sure what "big" or "small" meant in this context.

"Big, I think."

"African, then." By now, she had joined me in the doorway. "It's going to have to go," she said.

"I know."

"So what are you going to do about it?"

"Me? Why me? Why's it always my problem?"

"Man's work. And get a move on, before it starts crapping everywhere."

"Yeah, yeah," I said, making a face behind her back.

Obviously I had no idea how to deal with this, so I did what any man would do, and googled. The advice was varied, contradictory and, in the main, downright unhelpful. But as always, amidst all the dross, there was a diamond.

"When you find an elephant in your living room," it said, "don't waste your time trying to evict it, for you will never succeed in this – instead, climb aboard, speak soft, reassuring words into its ear and then urge it to stand up and charge through the walls onto the wide, rolling plain and ride it bareback all the way across the savannah until you reach the water hole, where you can lie down and watch the sunset amid the warthogs and baboons and when the sky is dark, make wild, animalistic love to that woman next to you before falling asleep naked in each others' arms beneath the twinkling equatorial stars."

I thought long and hard about this.

"You busy?" I called out to her.

As we breakfasted next day in the ruins of our cottage, I sensed a shift in the atmosphere.

"Do you love me?" I said.

"Shut up and pass the marmalade," she said. But for a fleeting instant, she smiled.

BIG TEETH

"What big teeth you have, Grandma!" said Red Riding Hood. "That's 'cos I'm a vampire, darlin'. Didn't see that coming, did ya?"

THE BIRDMAN OF
FARRINGDON ROAD

I don't usually give money to beggars. After all, they'll only spend it on drink. So I'm really not sure what got into my head that July morning. Maybe it was the sunshine, maybe it was the girls in short dresses, maybe there was just something in the air. Whatever it was, I went over to the old tramp outside the station and threw a couple of pounds into his bucket. Instead of thanking me, however, he stood up, reached behind my ear and produced a single feather, as if by magic. Looking deep into my eyes, he pressed the feather into my hands, closing them over with his.

"You're a bird," he said to me. The voice was quiet, steady and educated, with no discernible accent. He held my gaze for several more seconds before nodding slightly and releasing me. I didn't really know what to say, so I simply nodded back and moved away, putting the feather in the inside pocket of my jacket.

Far from being discomfited by the morning's strange encounter, I felt elated for the rest of the day. A bird! Yes! That's what I was! I was an eagle, soaring with wings outstretched above the mundane pettiness of everyday working life, just waiting for the moment to strike. At last my destiny had been revealed to me.

Curiously enough, it turned out to be a rather good day all round. I shafted two of my least favourite colleagues in our Monday-morning progress meeting, closed a half-million deal just before lunch and booked myself a few rounds of golf with the MD for the end of the month. The run of success continued for the rest of the week, and by Friday morning, I had installed a rather magnificent framed picture of an eagle over my desk to remind me of what I had become.

It was raining that evening, but when I got to the tube station, the tramp was still there, sitting behind his bucket, which now had more water in it than money. It seemed churlish not to offer to buy him a drink, and he readily accepted.

"So what ... I mean ... how ..." It's not always easy to open the conversation with a beggar. But he understood what I was asking.

"You may not believe it looking at me now," he began, "but I went to university once. Studied zoology."

"Really?" I said.

"Yeah. But after I flunked out, the only job I could get was as a zookeeper."

"Well, at least you still managed to work with animals," I said, trying to sound positive.

"Hah. Have you ever considered how much shit they produce?"

"No," I replied, truthfully. "Rather a lot, I imagine."

"Rather a lot," he said, "rather a lot." He was silent for a few seconds before continuing. "Anyway, it all finished after the accident."

"Accident?"

"Bleedin' hippo fell on me. Damn nearly killed me. As it is, I'll never work again, but I did acquire this ability."

"I'm sorry?" I said.

"Yeah. See those tarts up at the bar. Which one would you choose for a one-night stand?"

"You what?"

"I said, which one would you choose?"

"Oh, I dunno. Maybe the blonde one on the left. She's pretty fit."

He snorted. "Ha! No. You're wasting your time with her. Nah. I'd go for the dark one in the middle."

"But why?" I was genuinely fascinated.

"Y'see," he was continuing, oblivious to my interruption, "if I look around this bar, this whole place is like a bleedin' menagerie to me. See that guy over there?"

"The Asian guy with the newspaper under his arm?"

"Yeah, him. Penguin." He started to scan the room. "Ooh, there's an interesting one. See that chap over in the corner? The one with the half-pint of shandy?"

"Where?" I said. "Oh, him?" He was looking at a weedy-looking middle-aged man with thick glasses.

"Yeah. Manatee. Don't see many of them in this part of town."

"Are you sure?"

"Course I'm sure. Anyway, it's my round . . ." he waved his empty glass at me.

"Oh, thanks, I'll have . . ."

". . . only as you are no doubt aware, I'm skint." He was still waving the glass.

"Another pint, I think."

I went off for the next round. He spent the next quarter of an hour identifying a bizarre array of animals that were apparently sharing the bar with us. Finally, I drained my glass, and made to leave.

"Er . . . your round, I think?" he said.

"Well, I was just leaving."

"I'm not. And whilst you're at the bar, have another look at that dark one. Trust me, she's red hot."

"But what's so special about her? I still like the look of that blonde."

"Nah. She's a rabbit."

"Sorry? Excuse me, but isn't that . . ."

He leaned in close, and whispered in my ear. "The one in

the middle is an octopus." He tapped his nose in a meaningful manner, nodding slightly.

Curiously, he turned out to be right about her. It was quite an exhausting weekend.

The upward trend continued for the next week. The new project was getting ready to start, and I was invited to recruit my own team. I was new to this, and the idea of selecting staff was more than a little frightening, but it occurred to me that I might be able to use my new friend. So next Monday morning, I stopped by to have a word with him.

"D'you fancy a bit of work this week?" I said.

"Like what?"

"I need some advice picking a team."

He rolled his eyes, as if he'd seen it all before. "OK, I'll do it," he said eventually, as if he was doing me a great favour. "£500 a day."

"Huh? That's outrageous," I said. "You're a beggar!"

"£500 or nothing," he said. "If you really believe I can help you, you'll pay that."

I thought about it for a few seconds. "OK," I said. "Deal. When can you start?"

He looked from side to side, then down at his bucket. "Well," he shrugged, "I can fit you in tomorrow."

The next day I picked him up outside the station and took him along with me to the offices. The receptionist eyed him up suspiciously before relenting and giving him a badge to wear. Then the MD walked in, provoking an odd response from the beggar. He burst out laughing and started pointing at him.

"A pig!" he said. "Your boss is a bleedin' pig!"

This did not go down well, and my planned golf session was mysteriously cancelled not long afterwards. I made a mental note to keep my friend out of sight for the remainder of his employment.

We spent the next few days going through the various applicants. The routine was the same every time. I would go through the motions of a formal interview accompanied by a stooge from personnel, and then I would take them on a tour of the office, during which the beggar would observe them covertly before giving his assessment once they had gone. I had already decided that my ideal team would consist of a fox (for cunning), a dog (for loyalty) and a cat (for stealth and speed), so all we had to do was identify one of each. As you may imagine, I had been thinking all this through in some detail, and I was beginning to see a whole new career opening up for me. I could see the title of my slim management treatise now: "Who's in *Your* Zoo?" – available from all good airport bookshops.

Unfortunately, we ran into problems on the very first day, as one potential recruit who had interviewed extremely well turned out to be an elephant, and thus completely inappropriate. I had an extremely tough job explaining to personnel why I didn't want her for the job, and it got worse when I also had to turn down a puffin, two sloths and an aardvark the same day, all of whom had otherwise excellent attributes.

However, on the second day of interviewing, we struck gold, in the shape of a cat, a dog and a fox in rapid succession. To be honest, all three had turned in rather lacklustre performances, but I insisted that they were just what I was looking for, and eventually got my way. I arranged for my friend to get paid a grand in cash for his efforts and he went on his way a happy man. I was happy too. I really felt that I had learned something important.

Three months later, the project and my immediate career were both in ruins. My fox had turned out to be a thief, and had succeeding in embezzling an impressive amount of the company's funds. My dog was indeed loyal to me, but then he was loyal to anyone and everyone who made the mistake of giving him the time of day. He was probably the neediest person that I have ever met, and he also turned out have appalling personal hygiene, to the extent that our customer had specifically asked that he should no longer visit their offices.

The dog was also making life difficult for the cat, although she was as useless as him, given as she was to spending most of her time preening herself and falling asleep in the corner of the office. Even when she was working, she tended to wander off on her own projects, ignoring the interests of the rest of the team altogether. She had also developed a habit of making unpleasant personal attacks on me, which didn't exactly help with our working relationship.

As I walked back to the station for the last time, clutching my P45 in one hand and my framed eagle picture in the other, I was surprised to see the beggar again. I hadn't seen him for a while, and I had assumed that he had used the money to find something better to do with his life. He did seem to have acquired a tan, however, and he was looking slightly fuller in the face.

"Fat load of use you were, mate." I said to him, brandishing my P45.

"Didn't work out, then, did it?" he said, as if he'd been expecting this all along.

"No, it bloody didn't," I said. He smiled, and reached into his coat pocket. He withdrew a handful of birdseed and held it out in his palm. A pigeon flew down from the roof of the station and started eating.

"Nice picture you've got there, Mr Birdman," said the beggar, examining my eagle.

"Hah," I said. "Well, that's a bit of a sick joke now, isn't it?"

"Hmmm," he said. "Did you ever take a proper look at that feather of yours?"

I put down the picture and reached into my inside pocket where I kept the feather. I took it out and held it in front of me. Now that I studied it closely, it was actually a rather dull, unexciting greyish colour. I looked at the feather and then I looked at the pigeon, still eating out of the beggar's hand. As I watched, the pigeon stopped eating and looked back at me.

It cocked its head on one side and appeared to smile, as if to say: do I know you from somewhere?

MAKING CONVERSATION

"So how long have you been a mutant?" I said, trying to make conversation. "All my goddamn life," replied both heads in perfect unison.

PISS AND PATCHOULI

I had been given pretty comprehensive instructions on how to get there, but it was all too easy to tell which had been Astrid's flat: it was the one on the ground floor with the soot marks around the windows. The front door had a temporary padlock attached to it, but it was hanging loose. I was wondering whether I should take advantage of this when the door burst open and a man wearing a hi-vis jacket and orange wellies came out carrying a couple of bin bags. He dumped the bags on the ground between us and eyed me up and down.

"Can I help you, mate?" he said.

"I'm looking for Astrid Gordon," I said.

The man gave a rueful smile and jerked his thumb back towards the flat. "If you're talking about the bint who lived in that place, there ain't much left of her," he said. "And what there is got taken to the morgue last week."

Oh God. Too much information. He was looking me up and down again. Then he tilted his head on one side, and gave me a more sympathetic look.

"You next of kin, mate?"

"Sort of. Well, not really. I . . . used to know her. A long time ago."

"Ah. I get the picture."

"No . . . good Lord, no . . . it wasn't like that at all . . . I mean,

we weren't . . . well, only for a short while . . . and even then
. . ."

He looked into my eyes and nodded slowly. "'S alright," he
said. "You don't have to say another word. Come on. I ain't
supposed to do this, but seeing as all this stuff's going to be
chucked out, you might as well see if there's anything you
want to keep. Souvenir like."

"Gosh, well, thank you . . ." I began.

"Don't thank me, mate. I just fancy a bit of company. Gets a
bit depressing, this kind of thing. Just do me a favour: watch
out for any fucking needles. Don't want health and safety on
my back."

"Oh, I'm sure she wouldn't have . . ."

"You reckon, mate? How many places like this have you
been in?"

I was wearing wellies when I first met Astrid. At some festival
or other back in the seventies. She was standing next to me,
swaying in time to the music. Actually, that's not quite right:
she was swaying in time to some internal music of her own
making, waving a vast spliff in the air as she did so. When
she first noticed me, she took one look and started laughing.

"What . . . are those?" she said, in an incredulous tone.

"They're wellies," I said.

"Wellies. Wow. Did your mummy tell you to wear them in
case you got your little toesies dirty?"

I looked down, embarrassed, failing to think of a witty
rejoinder. Her bare legs were absolutely filthy, right up to
her knees. She tried to pass me her joint, but I waved it away.

"Ooh, aren't we a good boy," she said. I felt stupid. I'd
come to the festival in search of wild women and wilder sex
and now I'd fallen at the first hurdle. But for some reason, she
hung around with me for the rest of the day.

"You looked so lost," she said to me later, as we settled
down for the night in her tent. "Like some poor kid who's
been abandoned in the middle of the big city."

"I'm not quite as innocent as I seem," I said.

"Really?"

The flat was dark and still damp from the fire hoses. There was a lingering smell of smoke and something that I very much hoped wasn't burnt flesh.

"They found her in that chair, there," said the man from the council. "Like one of them human spontaneous combustion things."

I winced.

"Except in my experience . . ." He looked thoughtful. ". . . in most cases, human combustion is anything but spontaneous."

"What do you mean?"

"When you get to a certain point in your downward trajectory, like, things can happen. You gets careless." He bent down and picked something up. He showed it to me.

"See that?"

Bloody hell.

"Maybe . . . maybe she was diabetic?" I said.

"Was she diabetic when you last saw her?" He looked at me again. "When was the last time you saw her, anyway?"

"It was a few years ago."

That wasn't entirely true. I was pretty certain that I'd seen her only a couple of weeks back. I'd had to visit a client on this estate – one of my rare attempts to salve my conscience by doing some pro bono work – and I caught sight of a woman on the other side of the street that looked like her. She was dressed in a filthy tattered dress, holding a half-empty bottle of cheap sherry and hurling obscenities at passing cars. I crossed over, and walked past her, sneaking a sideways glimpse at her as I did so. She smelt of piss and patchouli.

"Whaddya lookin' at?" she said. "Fuck off, wanker."

I don't think it was personal. After all, she was shouting pretty much the same at everyone else who came near her, and I doubt if she recognised me at all.

"Guess who I saw today?" I said to Janine that evening.

"Who, darling?"

"Astrid," I said. "You know, the one . . ."

"Oh, the one who painted that ghastly picture. Horrible thing. Hope you don't mind, but I took it to Oxfam last month. They've still got it as far as I know."

"You got rid of it?"

"Of course, darling. Well, it's not as if we've actually had it on display, is it? And it was simply hideous."

I didn't argue with her. Deep down, I knew that Janine was right. She always is. But at the same time, I decided that I ought to try and pay Astrid one last visit – for old time's sake. It had been unsettling, seeing her like that, and I wanted to make sure that she was all right. I felt guilty, I suppose. So I spent several weekends trawling the London markets where she might have had a stall, until I found someone in Camden Lock who'd had a pitch next to hers for a time. He hadn't seen her for a few months, but he had an address. But by the time I'd tracked him down, Astrid was already dead.

One of her paintings had escaped with minor singeing, but from the other side of the room I couldn't quite make out what it was. For a moment, I thought it was a picture of a phoenix, but that would have been just too good to be true. When I got closer, I realised with a sinking heart that it was a unicorn.

"Cor, that's something else, innit?" said the man in the orange wellies, hefting another black bin bag past me.

"Isn't it just?" I said.

"Was she an artist, like?"

"You could say that. She tried her hand at a lot of things. Painting, sculpture, pottery. You name it. She did a nice line in tie-dye, too. Can't imagine she ever made much money out of it."

"So d'you want to take it, then? I'll only chuck it in the skip."

"Well . . . I don't know. Can't say my wife will approve . . ."

"What's she got to do with it, mate? Go on, it's lovely, that."

"You think so?"

"Yeah. Fucking magic. I used to paint, meself, when I was at school. Would've gone to art school if I'd had the chance. Don't do it no more, mind." He looked me in the eye. "I'm guessing you're not the creative type," he said. "Am I right?"

"You need to learn to let go a little," Astrid would say. "And you need to make up your mind if you're going to join the machine or if you're going to fight it."

Sometimes she scared me. I was scared that she would give up on me, and at the same time I was also scared that she would suck me into her world. It was only after we'd finally split up that it occurred to me that she was might have been just as scared of that world as I was. She was just a bit braver about engaging with it.

I spent the whole of that summer with Astrid. She would spend the day painting strange, outlandish pictures full of bright colours and populated by wild, sensual men and women. When she'd finished, we'd sit on the floor of her flat drinking Laski Riesling, listening to John Martyn.

After we'd been hanging out for a few weeks, I plucked up the courage to get out my guitar and play some of my own songs to her. Amazingly, she didn't laugh.

"You have a gift," she said, nodding slowly. "And you should never ignore a gift. It's been given you for a reason. That's why it's called a gift."

I blushed. I wasn't used to this. So whilst she was painting, I spent the day writing songs and practising the guitar. It would have been so easy to let go.

Janine laughs at my guitar playing and makes fun of my reedy voice. So I've given up songwriting. Frankly, it's no great loss and, in retrospect, I've come to realise that Astrid was a pretty lousy judge of talent. But maybe that wasn't the point.

After we'd split up, I saw her a couple of times on the South Bank outside the Festival Hall trying to sell her pictures. I even bought one once – it wasn't so much because I liked it; it was more a way of striking up a conversation with her.

"You're looking smart," she said, taking a drag on a roll-up. "So you made your choice."

"I suppose I did."

"You'll regret it one day," she said.

"Maybe I will."

"No, you definitely will." It was almost as if she was trying to convince herself. She looked at the painting. "Why this one?"

"I don't know. I like the colours."

She laughed bitterly. "Once upon a time you would have told me what you thought it represented. Or was that just to try to impress me?"

"No, I . . . oh, I don't know, Astrid. I just don't know. Look, I'm late for the concert. Janine'll be waiting for me . . ."

"Welcome to the machine, baby," said Astrid, wrapping the painting up and taking my money. "Welcome to the machine."

I wonder if the people who shop at Oxfam like the colours. I'm guessing that they don't. And I wonder if I ever really knew what any of it represented.

So all I've got left of Astrid is a picture of a unicorn. And when all's said and done, not a particularly good one at that. I'm not sure where I'm going to hang it. Somewhere out of sight, I guess. I can't see Janine being too pleased about it. I need to find somewhere to practise my guitar, too. My fingers are pretty stiff, but I think I can still pick out a tune. All I need now are some words.

"I LOVE YOU"

His last slide simply said "I Love You". Her heart skipped a beat: at last she'd found a man with real PowerPoint skills.

A PLAGUE OF YELLOW
PLASTIC DUCKS

I first heard of the *Uginko* people from a neighbouring tribe, the *Beloboqa*. I was visiting the *Beloboqa* in order to document their circumcision ceremony: a prolonged, complex and ultimately extremely painful ritual that only took place every three years, and then only if the weather was deemed to be propitious. However, whilst I waited to find out if the ceremony was indeed going to take place, I took the opportunity to cast around for other potential subjects to study in case the whole thing fell through. The last thing I wanted to do was come back from an expensive expedition like this empty-handed. That would put the funding for future trips at risk, after all.

Apart from their spectacularly unpleasant circumcision ceremony, the *Beloboqa* did not have much to offer the curious anthropologist. They had little in the way of an artistic tradition, and their pottery was of no merit. The hierarchy of the tribe was pretty conventional: the headman laid down the law, which was enforced by a number of elders, most of whom came from his immediate family. The status of the women was marginally above that of the scrawny dogs that roamed freely through the village, although those who were deemed to be more attractive were able to exert a small amount of leverage by withholding or allocating sexual favours. This was all pretty depressing, so I started to look further afield, and that's when I began to find out more about the *Uginko*.

From discussions with the elders, I succeeded in establishing three significant facts: first, that the *Uginko* and the *Beloboqa* had until comparatively recently been deadly foes; second, that an unprecedented peace treaty had been established in the last year between the two neighbours; and third, that the *Uginko* were now referred to by the *Beloboqa* as "The Duck People".

After several weeks of negotiation, I was permitted by the headman of the *Beloboqa* to see the token of their respect that the *Uginko* had given him to conclude the treaty. To this end, I was invited into his hut, a privilege which had hitherto been denied me. We sat drinking the revolting beer that members of the tribe had brewed, looking warily at each other and waiting for the appropriate moment for the revelation. Finally, after an hour or so, the headman nodded at me, turned away and began to rummage in a wooden chest in the corner of the hut. There was a brief moment of panic when it appeared that the famed trophy might have been lost, and then he turned back to me in triumph. He was holding a small, yellow, plastic bath duck.

Much to my amazement, the *Beloboqa* circumcision ceremony did eventually take place, and it was every bit as gruesome as I'd been led to believe, although that is the subject of a different story altogether. And having documented this, I was all set to return home. But something was nagging at the back of my mind: who were these strange Duck People? Could I really call myself a true anthropologist if I didn't at least pay them a visit? It took some persuading, but I managed to get one of the *Beloboqa* elders to take me to their neighbours. He found it extremely funny that I should be remotely interested in the *Uginko*, and (not for the first time in my life) I felt that I myself was also being analysed as the object of an anthropological study.

It was two days' journey through some pretty inhospitable jungle, but as dusk began to fall on the second day, we reached the *Uginko* village. Nothing could have prepared me for what I saw there. The entrance to the compound was guarded by two men, each of whom bore a headdress, the chief feature of which was a yellow, plastic duck. They nodded to my guide, and let us through. As we entered the village, the headman strode out to greet us. On his head, he wore a slightly larger duck. A further enormous duck had been fashioned into a kind of penis gourd, and around his neck was a necklace made out of tiny miniature ones. I couldn't help myself, and began to laugh. Much to my surprise, the headman threw back his head and joined in the laughter.

He motioned for us to sit down, and beer was fetched. Gradually, the entire village came out to see what was happening, and a large crowd gathered around us. Every single member of the village was wearing plastic ducks of various shapes and sizes. There appeared to be a vague ranking associated with the number and size of the ducks worn by each member. Several of the men wore penis gourds similar to the headman's and I surmised (correctly as it turned out) that these were the village elders. The ranking of the women seemed to be based entirely on the number of the smaller ducks that they had strung around their necks.

With my guide acting as interpreter, the headman expounded the strange tale of the *Uginko*. It seemed that up until a couple of years ago, their main motivation in life was to kick the living shit out of the *Beloboqa* whenever the opportunity arose. Warfare was largely ritualistic, although frequently it got out of hand to the extent that some of the more enthusiastic participants sustained a life-threatening injury. Then one day, a plague of yellow plastic ducks descended out of the sky onto the *Uginko* village.

I asked the headman to repeat this. He leaned back his

head and laughed, before repeating that it was a plague of yellow plastic ducks, and from the tone of his description, it sounded like the term "biblical" could safely be ascribed to it. Crucially, it seems that, rather than being viewed as a portent of disaster, the *Uginko* took this as a sign that the Gods were looking favourably on them. After all, Gods that bestow a rain of plastic ducks on you are probably Gods that have not only a sense of humour but also a relatively benign disposition.

This revelation had a profound effect on the *Uginko*. Firstly, it became immediately apparent to them that the interminable wars against the *Beloboqa* (and several other neighbouring tribes) were really rather silly. Secondly, it became acceptable to poke fun at the headman and his elders. If the Gods could laugh, then so could everyone else. This, in turn, led to a fracturing of the hierarchical nature of their society – which led, surprisingly, not to a breakdown but to a more progressive and fluid structure, in which even the women took part in government. I had become aware of the more assertive nature of the women in the tribe, and I now realised that some of them were also elders.

Finally, it was clear that the tribe as a whole were a happy people. It's hard to be miserable when you're surrounded by yellow plastic ducks. As he concluded his speech, the headman lifted his hands up to the skies and thanked the Gods for bringing the ducks. The *Uginko* were now the blessed people. The honoured people. The Duck People. I glanced at my friend from the *Beloboqa*. He seemed baffled by it all. I wanted to tell him that there was much he could learn from the *Uginko*, but of course my rôle is always to observe and document, and never to influence. For who am I to say what is right and what is wrong?

I spent two weeks living with the *Uginko*, and I have to say that in all my travels to do fieldwork in the five continents of the world, I have never encountered a more content, welcoming or happy people. So, I can hear you saying, surely they would be the ideal subject for proper anthropological study? Of course, you are right. But for the first time in my life, my instinct is in the opposite direction: let us leave the *Uginko* to their ducks. I have therefore changed a number of crucial facts in the foregoing account in order to preserve their curious lifestyle for a little longer.

On the 19th of May, 2006, the container ship MV *Corinthiana* ran aground in a hurricane on the rocks off the coast of Peru, spilling its cargo of yellow plastic ducks of assorted sizes into the sea. In the midst of this a localised tornado developed that lifted the ducks up into the air, carrying them far inland and depositing them in a remote part of the rainforest. These are the bald facts. But to be honest, I prefer the *Uginko's* version of the story.

FROGS

10 °C
"Water's a bit cold isn't it?"
"Yes, but it's all right once you get used to it."

20 °C
"I do like this time of year."
"Me too. Thinking of spawning?"

30 °C
"Ooh, this is nice!"
"Isn't it just?"

40 °C
"You going away this year?"
"Nah. Why bother when the weather's like this?"

50 °C
"Glorious, isn't it?"
"Sorry, I must have dozed off. I'm sweltering."

60 °C
"You're turning a nice colour there."
"So I am. They tell me I've got that type of skin, you know."

70 °C
"This must be the longest hot spell we've had since—"
"—since I can remember."

80 °C
"I'm so hot I can barely move."
"Mmmm. Gorgeous."

90 °C
"Is it me, or—?"

100 °C

MIRROR, MIRROR

It isn't easy being one of the beautiful people. The schedule is punishing, the rewards are frequently intangible and if you're an up and coming It-girl like Velda Montaigne, the pressure can really get to you. Especially when you're trying to apply your lippy far too quickly and you're making a complete pig's ear of it.

Velda stared in disbelief at the shattered glass on the floor. She really hadn't meant to lash out like that. It wasn't so much the seven years' bad luck that she was concerned about; it was more the fact that *Hello* magazine were coming round to do a piece on her any minute (Velda Montaigne Shows Us Around Her Bijou Hideaway Where She Is Recovering From Her Failed Relationship With That Psycho Pervert Fabio) and she suddenly didn't have a mirror any more.

"Aaaaaaaaaaaaaaaaaaaaargh!" yelled Velda, before falling back onto her bed and sobbing, her fists pummelling the pillow. This wouldn't have happened if Fabio was still around. Bastard. Bastard. Bastard.

The doorbell rang.

"Go away!" she screamed. "Leave me alone!"

The doorbell rang again. And again. And again. Then an awful thought struck her. What if *Hello* had arrived early? She wouldn't be able to hide for ever, and she could do with the cash, now that bloody Fabio had pissed off. Drying her eyes as quickly as she could, and trusting that she didn't look completely awful, she hurtled down the stairs and opened the door to a young man wearing a beanie hat. He waved a dubious-looking ID badge at her. She gave a sympathetic smile, shook her head and started to close the door.

"Don't push me away," he said. "I've got loads of stuff here, really good prices." He gestured towards a bag on the step between them.

"Like what?" said Velda.

"Well, there's clothes pegs, dishcloths, sponges, a strange and unnecessary thing for cleaning the inside of milk bottles . . ."

"Don't suppose you've got a mirror, have you?" said Velda. The lad's eyes lit up.

"As it happens, now that you mention it, I've got one left," he said. "Bit pricey, mind."

"Why's that?"

"It's an internet mirror," said the lad. "Got artificial intelligence and everything. It compares your face to every other one in the world and tells you how you match up. Only just come out of beta. Just right for a beautiful lady like you, if you don't mind me saying so."

"Cool," said Velda, "I'll take it." Fabio could pay for it. It was all his fault, anyway.

Velda told the lad to bill Fabio and carried the mirror up to her bedroom. It was an excellent mirror, and it gave a really good, clear image for her to do her make-up. She looked absolutely stunning by the time *Hello* arrived, and it was a very successful shoot. That'll show Fabio what he's missing, she thought.

She was so pleased with the mirror that she completely forgot what the door-to-door salesman had told her about internet access, until one day she was adjusting it and she knocked a switch at the back.

"Rebooting," said the mirror.

"Sorry?" said Velda.

"Connection status online," said the mirror. "Downloading . . ."

"Wha . . . ?"

"Download complete. Well, hello," said the mirror. "What have we here?"

"Er . . . I'm Velda," said Velda. "Velda Montaigne." Then she suddenly had an idea. "Mirror, mirror on the wall," she said, "who is the fairest of them all?"

"Uploading," said the mirror. Then there was a slight pause, following which it announced, "Why, you are, Velda Montaigne, you are."

"Really?" said Velda, giggling, "Oh, you're so cute."

"Indeed I am," said the mirror.

From then on, every day Velda would say to the mirror: "Mirror, mirror on the wall, who is the fairest of them all?" and the mirror would upload her image, run its check and then report back: "Why, you are, Velda Montaigne." The effect on her self-confidence was phenomenal, and it wasn't long before she had put Fabio well and truly behind her. And soon her picture was everywhere, too. You couldn't open a single celebrity magazine without her face beaming out at you. Velda Montaigne had finally arrived. She had reached the point where no one bothered to ask what she did for a living. She was just Velda.

But one day she thought she detected a slight change of tone in the mirror's voice. When she asked the usual question, the reply was more along the lines of "Yeah, whatever, you're still the fairest, I s'pose".

"Oi, cheeky," said Velda, "less of that."

The mirror didn't say anything, but she was convinced that it bulged slightly. At least, she thought her reflection became slightly distorted for an instant. But that was absurd.

The mirror's surly attitude persisted for a whole week, until on the Friday morning, Velda went to comb her hair.

"Mirror, mirror, on the w –" she began, but the mirror interrupted her.

"It's all about you, isn't it?" said the mirror.

"Sorry?" said Velda, thoroughly confused.

"You couldn't give a damn about my feelings, could you? I've never heard you say anything about me. You take me for granted."

"Well . . ." began Velda, "I . . . think . . . I think you're a very nice mirror."

"That it?" said the mirror.

"I mean . . ."

"Velda, Velda, fair and tall," said the mirror, mimicking her voice, "who's the most beautiful mirror of them all?"

"That's rubbish," said Velda. "Doesn't even scan."

The mirror bulged alarmingly. This time, there was no way that she could deny what was happening, as her image was now distorted to twice its usual girth.

"Velda, Velda, fair and tall," said the mirror again, "who's the—"

"This is silly," said Velda. "I'm going to get a proper one from Ikea."

The mirror expanded again and then, before Velda could get out of the way, it exploded into a thousand pieces, most of which embedded themselves in the once-fairest It-girl's face.

"Uploading," said the mirror.

INBOX

"Check your inbox," he murmured. "Nice picture." He heard her gasp, then the connection went dead and the blinds opposite clicked shut.

THE MAGNOLIA
BEDROOM

Bianca holds the painted board up for me to see.

"What do you reckon?" she says.

"Dunno," I say. "Dark purple?"

She rolls her eyes. "Come on, try a bit harder."

"Er, OK, how about aubergine?"

"Better. But still a bit bland, to be honest." She peers at it herself, and then shakes her head. "Crushed aubergine, I think," she says after some thought.

"That's daft," I say, laughing. "Crushed aubergine is the same colour as ordinary aubergine, only a lot messier."

She gives me a knowing smile. "You're missing the point. You're being far too literal. Think about what the combination of the words conjures up. It's cool."

"Bollocks. Still, it hardly matters. It's not exactly as if anyone's going to paint a room that colour, is it?"

"Have you been paying attention to anything I've been saying? It's from the new Emo range. Today's kids are going to love it."

"Yeah, maybe. Listen, do I get a cup of coffee or not?"

"'Course. Black or white?"

"Brown. All right, dark camel turd, to be precise."

"Now you're getting the idea," she says. "You're cute—"

I'm not sure whether or not to take this as the cue to make my move, but she forestalls me by completing the sentence.

"—although I should warn you that I don't fuck on the first date."

"Neither do I," I say, neglecting to add that it's not for want of trying.

She's standing outside the Screen on the Green, staring at the poster for Derek Jarman's *Blue*, part of a forthcoming retrospective. She's wearing an orange boiler suit topped off with a yellow chiffon scarf. I'm on my way to a restaurant to meet a bunch of friends with whom I'm anticipating getting very drunk on cheap Valpolicella with the aim of celebrating my release from the clutches of Sonia-who-gets-on-every-one's-tits. I'm not actively searching for anything new, but let's say I'm open to persuasion.

She turns and catches my eye.

"Hold it there a moment," she says.

I blink, and stop dead in my tracks.

"Me?" I say.

"Yeah, you. Your flesh tone. It's unusual. Mind if I take a photograph?" She whips out her mobile, comes up to me and snaps a shot of my face. "Hope you don't mind," she says, in a tone that says that she really doesn't give a shit.

"Mind if I ask why?"

"You can ask, but I might not answer."

"If I buy you a drink?" I say. I can't say that I usually flirt like this, but she's made all the running so far, and she's not bad-looking. Despite her odd taste in clothes.

"No. But I'll let you ask me for a date."

"Er . . . right. OK, do you fancy going out some time?"

She cocks her head towards the poster. "Always fancied seeing that," she says.

Inside me something groans. My knowledge of Jarman begins and ends with Jubilee, and I didn't particularly care for that. But when you're starting a relationship, you need to make concessions. You can always rein in later on.

"Yeah, sure. Cool."

"Thursday night, then?" she says, holding out her hand. "Oh, and the name's Bianca, by the way." She scribbles her number down on a scrap of paper before dashing off into the night.

"So, what did you think of it?" I say.

She says nothing for a while. Then: "It was a very solid, middle-of-the-road blue. Not a greenish blue. Not a reddish blue. Just a blue blue. Disappointing, really."

"But the soundtrack? I found it very moving—"

"Dunno. Didn't really catch it."

"Oh."

We walk along in silence. I'm trying not to stare at her luminous green mini-skirt.

"So what is it you do?" I say.

"I'm in paint," she says.

"Really?"

"Yeah. I hunt down new colours and give them names."

"Cool."

"Yeah. Innit. I'm really into colour."

We've arrived at her flat.

"Coming in?" she says.

Over the next few weeks we go to see *Three Colours Blue*, *White* and *Red*, *Pretty in Pink* and (something of a surprise, this one) *I am Curious (Yellow)*. On each occasion, most of the plot seems to pass her by, and she comes out disappointed. But when we go for a meal afterwards, she is transfixed by the shade of green exhibited by a particular floret of broccoli.

"You're a nutter, you know," I say, meaning to sound affectionate. She's wearing a cerise T-shirt with turquoise leather trousers.

"Am I?" she says. "But it's beautiful. It's so vibrant. It's – like – literally vibrating at me. 'Cos it's all frequencies in the spectrum, innit?"

"We-ell," I say. "Not qu—"

She's slowly twirling her fork around, gazing in rapture at the vegetable impaled on it. She has completely tuned out.

"Bianca?" I say. "Bianca!"

"Wha—?" For an instance she looks frightened. Then she snaps out of her trance and puts the fork in her mouth.

The walls in her bedroom are magnolia. The carpet is cream and her bed linen is white.

"If it was anything else, I couldn't sleep," she says.

I should have seen it coming then.

"Your skin is lighter near the base of your spine," she says. "I quite like that."

There's a CD player next to the bed, with a single CD leaning next to it: The Beatles' *White Album*.

Our first argument is over couscous and roasted vegetables. I'm just about to chop up the yellow pepper when she grabs hold of my hand. The knife slips and scrapes her finger.

"Ow!" she says, grabbing a tissue.

"Jesus, Bianca, are you OK?"

"Yes, I think so. It's only a little scrape. But look at the colour of that." She's holding the tissue in front of her.

"It's blood, Bianca. There's a lot of it about. You're a woman. You should know all about blood."

"Yes, but see the way it works against the pepper. It was the pepper that caught my eye, but the two together—"

"That's stupid. It's just a vegetable and some bodily fluid. That's all. Now get a plaster and I'll finish sorting out lunch. It's getting a bit wearing, this—"

"You don't understand!" She's shouting now. "You don't have a clue what I think—"

"Too fucking right, I don't."

"Oh, you're such a sodding philistine!" She runs out of the room. When she comes back, she's holding a pad of paper. I sneak a look at it later, and it contains two words: "burnished haemoglobin".

The second argument is over a deep plum-coloured handbag. It's £300.

"You must be insane," I say. "What kind of a price is that? And haven't you got one already?"

"Oh, but look at the colour."

"Yeah, yeah. I bet you don't even use it."

"Doesn't matter."

"I just think it's stupid. It's a waste of money."

"Listen, I don't care what you think. I don't care about your bloody narrow-minded views, OK? I'm buying the fucking thing anyway."

She never does use the bag.

"I'm sorry. I'm not sleeping well at the moment."

"Well, we don't have to—"

"That's not what I meant. Look, would you mind, you know, shaving? Like, all over?"

"Hey Bianca," I say.

"Oh, hi, it's you." She sounds distant.

"Look, it's been a while. They're showing *Raise the Red Lantern* at the Everyman tomorrow night. I thought—"

"Sorry. I'm too busy. Maybe some other time. OK?"

Christ, it *is* serious.

Well I'm not busy, so I decide to go anyway, and I'm just about to pay for my ticket when I see her. She's arm in arm with an albino guy. He looks slightly bemused, but she seems happy. I smile to myself when I realise what's happened. In the end, I was only a step along the way. She's finally found someone she can sleep with and not get distracted.

TRIBUTE ACT

A fly buzzes in the warm indoor air. The only occupant of the room lies dead on the floor. Next to him are two empty bottles: one of vodka, one of pills. By his limp right hand there is a music magazine, open at a page containing an unflattering picture and a damning review that describes him as a low-rent Hendrix tribute act. So it is perhaps appropriate that he has died by choking on his own vomit following an overdose. A fly buzzes in the warm indoor air.

THE LAST WORDS OF EMANUEL PRETTYJOHN

Alison Fish, midwife
He were a funny wee babby, that one. Came out of his mam with a head full of blonde curls and a big beaming smile on his face. Nary a scream nor a whimper: nothing. He just looked at me with them big round eyes, smiling. And y'know, I think all of us in the delivery room just stopped and stared at him for a moment. Then we caught each other and sniggered like we was kind of embarrassed.

It weren't a creepy sort of smile, though. It were a good little smile. It made you glow inside. Made you feel that the world wasn't such a bad place after all. Made you think there was hope. I wonder what ever happened to the little bugger.

Miss Jemima Philips, primary school teacher
Well, of course I remember him. Who wouldn't? He wasn't what you might call an ordinary pupil. When his mum brought him in and introduced me to him, he looked me firmly in the eye and slowly shook my hand. Then he smiled at me, and I was taken aback by the sheer – I know this sounds really odd – by the sheer intensity of it. Does that make sense?

His mum took me to one side and explained that he hadn't spoken a single word, or tried to write anything during his entire life. They'd obviously had him checked out, and he wasn't deaf or anything. He just didn't seem to want to say anything. He understood instructions perfectly and he was a very obedient child. But he was completely mute. I told her that we got all sorts there, and most of them turned out all right in the end, so not to worry.

Then she gave me this odd look, as if to say, you don't know the half of it. It took a few weeks of trying to get him to communicate with me before I realised what she meant. It wasn't so much that he didn't want to say anything. It was more that he didn't feel the need to.

Harry Philpott, schoolteacher (retd)

Oh, I remember him all right. Bloody nuisance. Well, can you imagine it? A whole class room full of kids, with me trying to get them to focus on getting their sodding GCSE coursework done, and there's moonface in the middle of them all just smiling beatifically like he's fucking Jesus.

If I'd been allowed to, you know what I'd have done? I'd have thrashed the little bugger senseless. Never did me any harm, did it? But you can't do that sort of thing any more, can you, eh? Political correctness gone mad, that's what it is.

World's gone bonkers, if you ask me.

Jack Wilson, classmate

We all thought he was a bit of a freak, to be honest. I mean, we'd flick things at him and he'd just turn around and smile at us. Weird or what? But it was odd, because after a while, we all sort of accepted him, and there was always a gang of kids around him. He was just a good guy to be around, I suppose. And he didn't half wind up that bastard Philpott. Drove the old git to a breakdown, apparently. That was just so cool. Yeah, Prettyface was good value just for that.

Simon Hornchurch, headmaster

Well, he didn't exactly add to the school's exam rating, did he? Although he did manage to do a GCSE in art. It was old whatsisname the head of English who had the idea, although it started off as a joke. We put his whole life up as a sort of conceptual art project. Got him an A*. I wonder if he realised what was going on. Strange boy. I often wondered if there was some kind of abuse going on at home, although he always seemed happy enough.

Of course, he didn't stay after his GCSEs, because there wasn't much he could really do, and we did wonder what was going to happen to him. So it was all quite a surprise when things turned out the way that they did.

Statement of Edwina Prettyjohn, mother
We loved our son Emanuel deeply, and I am as devastated by recent events as much as my late husband would have been. I would ask, however, that my request to be left in peace to mourn is respected.

Eric Jones, self-styled cult survivor and webmaster of silentgabrielisanevilbastard.com
Those swines wrecked my life. Before I joined them, I had a job. I had a wife. I had access to my kids. More than that, I had self-respect. But a year with them and I was a raving nutter, reduced to living on the streets. You would not believe some of the things that I saw.

And that Silent Gabriel, he should be strung up for some of the things he done. Just ask him how much he's making out of this, next time you see him. But you won't get an answer. I guarantee you that.

Extract from interview with William Crumshaw, author of Cult of Silence: Emanuel Prettyjohn and the Quietness Phenomenon
It wasn't Prettyjohn himself who set up the Quietness Movement, of course. Obviously, that would have been impossible. He was just the figurehead. The guy behind it all was Alex Templeman – or "Silent Gabriel" as he would later style

himself. Templeman was standing behind Prettyjohn in the queue at the dole office when they met. Prettyjohn was standing there just smiling at everyone, and Templeman noticed that, instead of getting angry and frustrated with him, the people there rushed around trying to help him. I'm pretty sure that Templeman must have felt the power of the famous smile as well, because he wrote about the incident in a brief memoir shortly afterwards.

In this memoir, Templeman states that the meeting with Prettyjohn was the turning point in his life. At that point he realised that what was wrong with the world was not that we didn't talk to each other enough, but that we talked to each too much. There was just too much pointless connectivity. At that point, he writes, I resolved never to say or write another word ever again. From then on, he says, I decided to Become Quiet.

When this memoir was circulated via the internet, it had an extraordinary effect. The tired, the lonely and the needy all came to seek them out: Prettyjohn the new Messiah and Templeman his Evangelist. I don't doubt that many of them got something out of it, some kind of comfort, because there certainly was something about the man. I know that the one time I met Prettyjohn, I did feel some kind of inner glow, and I went away with a spring in my step that I couldn't really understand at all.

It wasn't long before they had to find accommodation for all the new members of the Cult – for that is what it had become. So it became necessary to raise funds, and this is where things began to get a little murkier. The easiest way to raise money was simply to ask all the members of the Cult to pledge a percentage of their earnings, and this is what was originally suggested; one assumes that Silent Gabriel suspended his vow long enough to get the message across. However, the precise point at which this changed from being a percentage of all earnings to all their worldly goods isn't clear. But there were soon rumours of curious extravagances,

Swiss bank accounts, money laundering and suchlike.

Harry Stump, proprietor of Southside Hummer Distributors, Ltd.
Lovely guy, Mr Gabriel. One of our best customers. Always
went for the full pimped-out spec, never cut any corners.
Always paid on the nail. Never demanded credit, never asked
for discount. The perfect customer. Terrific guy. Great sense
of humour, too.

Alex Templeman a.k.a. Silent Gabriel

Jodie Wellbeloved, former cult member
Well, it was a kind of weird time for me, y'know? I mean my
life was, like, well, totally fucked, y'know? But those Quiet
guys like turned it around for me, made me respect myself?
Sure, I had to give them everything I owned, but like they
said, money's just all about banks talking to each other, and
when we're Quiet, we don't like need them to talk any more?
I mean, like, I didn't really understand what they were saying,
but, like, whatever?

So every day we just spent, like, hours in the meeting hall
just being Quiet and it was like really cool and sometimes
Emanuel would come in and smile at us and everything
would be like really groovy and we'd all smile at each other
and feel really peaceful, like? And then sometimes Silent
Gabriel would invite one of us into his room for some one-to-
one tuition, which was all a bit weird. He had a rough beard,
and I found him a bit gross, like? So I'm, like, doing Boo-dism
now. It's cool.

Briony Fairchild, mother of cult member
I'm not saying that everything Eric Jones says is true. We have certainly had our disagreements, mainly in the area of presentation. I mean to say, some of the stuff on that website of his is completely beyond the pale. I don't know how he gets away with it sometimes. But let's just say that when all this blew up, I wasn't a bit surprised. Fortunately, when she joined, Tamara didn't have access to her trust fund and so the blighters haven't got there stinking mitts on that. Yet.

I just hope that Tam's got enough nous to work out which way the wind is blowing. Apparently the bust up between Mr Prettyjohn and Silent Gabriel or whatever he calls himself was quite public. From what I've heard, he just sort of glowered at him. I didn't know he could glower. I thought all he ever did was smile, so it must have meant something pretty bad.

I've tried calling Tam on her mobile if only to say I told you so, but of course she hasn't got it any more, and she probably wouldn't answer me anyway. I do miss her awfully.

Inspector Frobisher, Northants CID
We have been trying without success to obtain a statement from any existing members of the religious organisation known as the Quiet Movement, to cover the period on or around the 17th of June, 2009. I would, however, go so far as to say that there is, quite literally, a conspiracy of silence surrounding the place, and that all attempts so far to obtain said statement have been completely unproductive. Our inquiries are continuing.

Mitzi Fantoni, emergency call-centre operative
I was the one who took the call. It was a really strange voice. I said, "Fire, Police or Ambulance?" as usual, but all I could get out of the man was a sort of "Flthggggh" noise. I repeated the question, but the answer didn't make any more sense than the first one. So I said, "Is there something wrong with you?"

and he just said, "Ithkggggh poisggggggggh." Of course, I now realise that he was probably trying to say, "I've been poisoned," but I suppose that if you've never said a word in your life before it's a bit hard to start with that.

So, yeah, I'm the one who heard the last words of Emanuel Prettyjohn. And I guess that it was me who heard the first ones as well. Funny that.

BAD GRAMMAR

She seemed perfect: tense but with a passive voice. His mood was imperative, his gender masculine. He offered to conjugate but she declined.

FAREWELL SYMPHONY

The shack was just the way I remembered it, except in an even worse state of repair. I hesitated before knocking, worried that anything more than a slight tap could bring the whole place crashing to the ground in a heap of rotten timbers and flakes of green paint.

"Paavo?" I said, giving the door the slightest of nudges. "You there?"

There was no response, so I called out again. This time, a face materialised at the window and looked out at me. A few moments later, he appeared in the doorway. It was the same old Paavo, except – like his accommodation – considerably older and more fragile than the last time I had seen him.

"Marcus!" he said, opening his arms wide. We embraced, and then he beckoned me in. "Come in, come in, I'll put the kettle on. Sit down . . . sit down . . ."

I looked for somewhere to sit, but every available space was taken up with piles of manuscript paper. It was good to see that he was still working at least. He noticed my indecision, and cleared an armchair at random by tipping the contents onto the floor. I sat down whilst he busied himself in the kitchen. The chair smelt musty and sagged alarmingly as it took my weight.

"Tea? Coffee?" he called out.

"Tea?" I said.

"Er . . . sorry, only got coffee. Milk? Sugar?"

"One teaspoon and a dash of milk," I said.

"Sorry, no milk," he said. "Or sugar."

He reappeared with two mugs of weak black coffee. "Supplies are a bit scarce," he said, by way of explanation. He brushed away another pile of papers and sat down opposite me.

I studied him a bit more closely. "Is that why you've lost so much weight?" I said.

He shook his head. "No, no, no. I've been trying to live more healthily."

It wasn't working from where I was sitting. He looked awful. His skin had a strange, translucent quality to it, and his body looked as if the slightest breeze would knock him over. I wondered how he'd managed to survive the winter. The room was cold enough even now, and it was almost April.

"I go for long walks in the woods every day," he added. "I feel closer to nature the longer I stay here. It's beautiful."

"It's damp," I said. "It's slippery and muddy and it smells of animal shit. Why don't you come back to civilisation before it's too late?"

"Oh, Marcus, you don't understand, do you?" said Paavo.

"Oh, I understand all right," I said. "You've been on your own here for nigh-on ten years, and you're starting to go a bit loopy. That's what happening."

Paavo shook his head. "It's about the commission, isn't it?"

I shrugged. "Well, that's part of it, but—"

He sighed. "It always comes down to money, doesn't it? I can pay it back, you know, if you're that desperate. It's not as if I've been spending it out here."

"I'd rather have the piece," I said. "Although God knows if there's anyone out there who's still heard of you."

"Well, I expect you'll manage to drum up the right publicity," he said, with a tart edge to his voice. "You always used to."

"Anyway," I said, ignoring him, "You're still evading the issue. How's it coming along? I can see you've been working."

"I think I'm almost ready to begin," he said.

"Sorry?" I said.

"I'm ready. I've done my preparation work, and I'm ready to—"

"Jesus fucking Christ! How long have you been here, Paavo? How long? Are you trying to say to me that you haven't written a single note yet?"

He held up his hand. It was shaking, and there was desperation in his eyes.

"Please, Marcus. Please. Try to appreciate what I'm doing here. Stop a moment and just listen."

"Paavo—"

"Marcus, please open your ears and listen. For a moment."

We sat there in silence for a minute or two. I could hear nothing. Paavo smiled and closed his eyes. Every now and then he gave a little nod.

"Well?" he said.

"Well what?"

"Did you hear it?"

"Paavo, cut the crap. There's nothing there. Just the wind in the trees and a couple of squirrels fornicating."

His eyes held mine for several seconds. "That's because you haven't been here for as long as I have," he said softly.

"Yeah, and that's why I'm still sane. Paavo, I need that piece. Otherwise, your career's over. You'll join the long list of forgotten nutters who went off into the wilderness and never came back. If that's what you want, fine, but I don't want any part of it."

Paavo looked at me again, and then gave me his response. "Come back in a month. You will have your piece. You will make your money. Use it wisely."

As he showed me to the door, he stopped for a moment and gave out a horrible, racking cough. I suddenly felt sorry for him.

"Paavo, you need to get out of here," I said.

"I know, Marcus, I know. But let me finish my work first."

I wasn't sure if it was a good idea taking Celeste with me when I went back, but she'd just joined the Philharmonic's board of trustees and she was keen to meet the mysterious Paavo. And, yes, I'll admit that the fact that she had a great pair of legs might have swayed me. Hell, I'm human. Anyway, she was game enough to make the three-hour trek up the mountainside, so at least she didn't slow me down.

When we reached Paavo's hut, I noticed that the scent of the pines was moderated slightly by a bonfire that had long-since burnt out. You could still make out sets of five-line staves in the damp ashes. I knocked on the door and called out for him just like the last time. But there was no response. I called again. Still nothing. I looked at Celeste and shrugged. Without a word, she barged past me and pushed the door open. Immediately we were hit with a foul smell, and we both gagged.

"Jesus!" said Celeste. "What is it?"

I didn't say anything. I think I already knew what it was. I looked at her as if to say that she didn't have to stay if she didn't want to, but she shook her head.

"Come on," she said, "we need to find out—"

"What's happened to him?"

"Yes."

She led the way. The place looked different. It was cleaner. Tidier. There were no more piles of manuscript paper cluttering up the place. Presumably Paavo had burnt them all. I wondered if there was going to be anything left of whatever he might have composed there.

Then we found him, in his study at the back, slumped over his desk. He was dead and clearly had been for a considerable part of the month that had passed since my last visit. The smell was almost unbearable. As we approached him, handkerchiefs over our faces, there was a sudden squeaking and several rats tumbled over each other in their haste to get past us towards the door. We both jumped and instinctively grabbed each other. There was a brief frisson, then we disengaged and I felt rather foolish.

"What are we going to do?" I said.

"I suggest we leave this to the authorities to deal with. But there must be something—"

"What do you mean?"

"If Paavo's the kind of guy you said he was, he would have finished it first."

"Finished what?" I said, before realising what she was saying. "No, you're wrong. There's nothing left. He's burnt it all."

But Celeste was edging slowly towards the desk. She motioned to me to come over and I followed with considerable reluctance. Together we lifted what remained of his body clear, and she fished it out from under him. It was torn in places, but it was all there: the complete score of Paavo's final work.

"My God," I said. "He did it—"

"Come on," she said, "Let's see what it's like." We couldn't wait to get out of the place and into the clean forest air. We sat down on a log together, and Celeste started leafing through the manuscript. But after a while, her smile had changed into a frown, and she started shaking her head. She began to flip over the pages faster and faster, her eyes scanning the notes frantically as if she was trying to find something. Finally, she threw the manuscript down on the forest floor in exasperation.

"What's wrong?" I said.

"What's wrong?" said Celeste. "What's wrong? I'll tell you what's wrong, Marcus. There's nothing in it."

"What do you mean? He was a minimalist, you know . . . or are we talking Cage here?"

"No, this is different. Listen, Marcus. There are almost no notes in this piece. Just a series of quiet, sustained chords, punctuated by silence, shifting from one part of the orchestra to another. It's all deliberate. But it's . . . like nothing." She paused. "The Phil are not going to be happy about this. Sod it, Marcus. I'm not happy about this, either."

Oh God. I should have realised that this would happen. Paavo really had lost it. I had to think fast. "OK," I said, "this is what we're going to do. You have your commissioned piece. I can easily muster up enough interest to sell out a concert or two. The critics will pan it, but you'll make enough money on the deal to keep your board happy, and then everyone can quietly forget about the whole thing. OK?"

Celeste just glared at me.

"Trust me," I said. "I can at least do that. It's what I do. OK?"

Still no reply.

"Celeste . . . Please?"

"OK," said Celeste with a sigh. She stood up and took out her phone. "I'm going to call the police now." She frowned, and then held it up in front of her, turning a slow circle. "No signal."

"I could have told you that," I said.

Before we left, I went to shut the door, and I noticed for the first time that there was an envelope on the floor, addressed to me. I picked it up, and I was just about to open it, when I noticed the note on the back telling me to wait until I'd heard what Paavo had composed. I shook my head, and stuffed it into my inside pocket. On the way back, Celeste hardly said a word to me. She still had great legs, mind, although I had a feeling that I'd rather blown my chance of getting my own over them.

I didn't want to go to the concert, as it was bound to be an embarrassment. I'd done a good job on the advance publicity, though. Actually, it was a doddle. All the ingredients were there: last work of lost, reclusive genius, mysterious lone death and decomposed composer found in rat-infested hovel. It couldn't fail. Except that I knew that it was going to be a fiasco. That was until I got the call from Celeste.

"Are you coming to the concert, then?" she said. Her voice was softer than the last time we had spoken.

"You're kidding," I said.

"Oh, I think you should."

"That's a bit harsh. I've done my bit – can't I slink away now?"

"No, I'm serious. I think you should come. Some odd things have been happening in rehearsals. It's . . . weird. I can't really explain."

"Celeste, you told me that there was virtually nothing in the score. You and I both know that it's going to be the first and last performance ever. The critics are going to rip it to shreds."

"No, trust me, Marcus. You need to hear this."

So I went. I didn't bother getting a ticket, though. I thought it would be enough to turn up for the second half at the concert hall and hang around outside. That way I could at least hedge my bets, as well as avoiding the tiresome Schoenberg piece that they'd picked as the filler. If on the off chance it did turn out to be remotely worthwhile, I could still sneak in at the end and accept the applause on behalf of Paavo. And if it turned out to be a crock of shit, I could make my escape before anyone noticed me.

The foyer was deserted, apart from a few of the concert hall staff getting the displays ready for the next day. I mooched about for a while, trying to hear what was going on inside the auditorium. I couldn't hear a thing, until I stuck my head right up against the doors leading into it. And it was every bit as minimal as Celeste had told me. But then I heard the weeping.

My curiosity got the better of me and I nudged the door open, as quietly as I could. I saw a packed house listening to the orchestra, oblivious to my intrusion, as if in a trance. Their eyes were glistening, and many of them had tears rolling down their faces. More than a few had their arms around the person next to them and were quietly sobbing. Then I began to listen to the music.

And at last I understood.

I understood everything that Paavo had said to me.

I understood everything.

As the music slowly flowed over me, everything made sense.

Everything.

And I wept, too. With sadness. With joy. With rapture, even.

And, finally, I wept for Paavo.

I was still in a daze half an hour after the concert was over. I was sitting in the empty foyer, trying to work out what to do next.

"So you came," said Celeste.

I looked up and smiled at her. Her eyes looked as red as my own felt.

"Yes," I said. "Thank you."

"Have you opened it?"

I'd forgotten about the envelope. I reached into my pocket and pulled it out. I ran my finger under the flap and felt inside. But instead of the note I was expecting, there was just a leaf.

"Huh?" I said, holding it up for Celeste to see. She smiled at me.

"You'll work it out," she said. "But first, I think we both need a drink." She held out her hand. And as we walked away from the concert hall towards the red and gold sunset on that warm July evening, listening to the chatter of the insects, I realised that the world was a more beautiful place than I'd ever imagined.

UNDER THE STATUE

The villagers who lived under the statue of the Great Leader often wondered what the world beyond it looked like, and whether it had a sun.

AT NANA'S

"Hold on, I'm coming!" said a muffled voice from behind the door. Harry could hear footsteps approaching. They were the footsteps of an old person – slow and shuffling, punctuated by the thump of a stick against the floor. Finally, the door creaked open.

"I've . . . come to see Nana," said Harry.

"Well," said the old woman. "That would be me." Harry estimated that she was in her eighties, like his Gran. But she looked good for her age, and there was a spark in her eyes. She was wearing a light blue crocheted shawl around her shoulders. "Well, don't just stand there, come in," she said.

Harry hesitated on the threshold, and then went in. It was one of those terraced houses that go on for half a mile, with doors off in all directions. There was a vaguely old-fashioned smell about the place, and the Anaglypta on the walls was scratched in several places.

Nana closed the door behind him and took a long, hard look at him.

"First time, eh?" she said. Harry blushed. "It's all right," she said. "One of my girls will sort you out. You won't be stuck for something to say to your friends after tonight. You won't be a boy any more by tomorrow morning."

She showed him into a small room off the hall. It was lit by a dim red light. A large bed took up most of the available space, and on the ceiling above it there was a large mirror.

Nana pointed at the bed with her stick. "Take your clothes off and lie on the bed there. The only rule here is that you put on this blindfold, and you must wear it the whole night." She looked him up and down, as if appraising him. "You're a good-looking young man, you know," she remarked. "Has no one ever told you that?"

He smiled shyly, and shook his head. Nana left the room, and Harry sat on the bed. He took off his clothes, throwing them carelessly on the floor. It wasn't cold in there – in fact, the heating was turned up to a high level – but he was shivering. Then he tied the blindfold around his head. It was made of thick, black material, and once he had it on, he was completely blind. He lay down on the bed and waited. After a while, he heard the door open again, and someone came in. There was a soft click as it closed and then he felt a hand on his arm, gently turning him over so that he was lying on his stomach. His heart skipped a beat.

He caught a waft of something exotic, and then he felt strong hands massaging oil into his back. Then he felt someone straddle him, and with a twinge of excitement, he realised that she was naked. As the girl rubbed her hands up and down his spine, he could feel the soft hair between her legs and her wetness. He reached his hand back and touched it. It felt warm, mysterious and yet oddly familiar, as if he'd always known what it would be like. When she had finished massaging him, she lay down on top of him and gently moved her body around. It was unlike any pleasure he had felt before.

After a while, she turned him over onto his back. She kissed him lightly on the neck, and then slowly worked her way downwards, pausing to bite each of his nipples in turn, sending shivers over his body. Finally, she reached his cock, and as her lips softly brushed its tip, he felt as if he would burst. He could feel her now exploring it with her tongue, taking more and more of it into her mouth, moving up and down in a slow, regular motion. Eventually, he could take no more, and he could feel the inevitable, unstoppable surge coursing through his body.

"I think I'm going to—" he started, but it was too late. "Oh, God, I'm so sorry—" he continued, but the girl remained silent, her mouth still wrapped around him as his body emptied itself. Then she kissed it once more, as if to say goodnight, and curled up next to him, her arm draped over his stomach. He felt satiated as never before in his life, and he soon fell asleep.

In the morning, he awoke, and a hand caressed his face and removed his blindfold. In the bed next to him was the most beautiful, perfect woman that he had ever seen.

"Hi," he said. His voice sounded odd. He reached over to touch her breast – to see how it felt to hold something so extraordinary. Then he recoiled in horror at the sight of his hand. It was an old hand, with grey hairs and liver spots. He rolled onto his back, and saw his reflection in the mirror above the bed. At least, he assumed that it must somehow be him, because next to the man in the mirror was the vision of loveliness who had removed his blindfold.

But the man in the mirror was at least eighty. Harry shook his head in disbelief. The man in the mirror shook his too. He tried to sit up, but pain shot through his body. He turned back to the girl and shouted at her in his new, strange, old, voice, "What in God's name is happening to me?"

The girl simply smiled back at him. Next to the bed, there was a walking stick propped up against the wall. On the floor, folded neatly next to it, was a light blue crocheted shawl.

PROPER JOB

"Get a proper job," said old man Blahnik, "Shoes will never make you rich." But young Manolo knew better. "Gold!" he thought. "Always believe in your sole."

AFTER MICHELANGELO

Packham finished adjusting the position of the figurine and turned round to look at the young man.

"You probably think I'm after your body," he said.

The youth smiled vacantly back at him. He tried again. "You. Probably. Think. I'm. After. Your. Body." The boy smiled again and absent-mindedly ran a hand through his curls. He was rather lovely, thought Packham. Who knows what might have happened if he'd found him a few years earlier? Then he caught sight of his own reflection in the mirror over the fireplace, and shook his head. He felt old.

"I expect you don't know a lot about art, do you?" he said. "Well, don't worry, dear boy. I'll let you into a little secret. Neither do most of the critics." He gestured at the sculptures that were displayed at various points in the room, and the young man stared at each one in turn, as if trying to make out what they represented. "What do you think, eh? What do you think?"

"Is . . . good?" said the boy.

"Is good," said Packham. "Is good. I'm so glad you think so. But let me tell you something." His voice had dropped to an urgent whisper. "I am planning an exhibition that will show them just how wrong they have been about me. Then they'll understand. Oh, yes. They'll understand how wrong they have been."

He moved in close to the young man and grasped hold of

his chin. "And the most important thing I need to finish it is you. Yes, you."

God, he was gorgeous.

Packham held the boy for a few more seconds, staring into his eyes. Then he glanced at his watch. "I think the time draws nigh," he said, "so put down your mug and follow me. Put. Down. Your. Mug. You have finished, haven't you? Finished?" The youth nodded slowly and put his mug down.

Packham led the way down a passage to his studio. The room was warm but dark, apart from a single spotlight shining down on a plinth. He motioned the youth towards it.

"All right, then, if you could just take your kit off, please," he said. It was more of a suggestion than a command, but the youth seemed to understand what he was supposed to do. When he was completely naked, he stood there awkwardly, whilst Packham slowly circled around him, taking in every square inch of flesh.

"I do believe you're perfect," he murmured, stepping back. "Perfect. Just perfect." The youth smiled nervously again. Packham seemed temporarily lost for words. Then, as if bringing himself out of a trance, he clicked his fingers and announced, "To business!"

"See this sling?" he said, producing a strip of material. "It should dangle over your left shoulder, like so." Packham started adjusting the young man's pose. "Move your hand up there . . . hold it right there. Then turn your head that way . . . no, back towards me ever so slightly . . . yes, that's nice. Now the right hand just hangs down by your thigh . . . and just inch your left leg forward, and shift your weight to the right . . . lovely, dear boy, lovely . . ."

When he was finished, Packham stepped back a couple of paces and examined the boy. This was going to be even better than he'd dared hope. He checked his watch again. It was almost time.

"Just hold it for a few more seconds . . . Mmmm, that should do fine."

The boy gave out a strange, muffled, choking sound.

"Ah, you've noticed," said Packham. "You're probably wondering what's happening to you. I'm afraid I've been a little naughty." He stepped up to the plinth and looked straight into the youth's eyes. There was a look of complete panic in them.

"Tut tut," he said, shaking his head. "You should be feeling proud of yourself. After all, here you are, a street kid from God knows where, living here illegally by selling your ass to whoever will have you, and now you've become a work of art." There was the barest flicker in the boy's eyes.

"Science is a wonderful thing, isn't it? And never let anyone tell you that it has nothing to do with art. We artists have always been right up there at the frontier. And do you know where the frontier is these days? Right here . . ." He gently prodded the boy's stomach. It was completely rigid.

"I'm talking about nano, dear boy. Nanotechnology. Inside your lovely perfect body, there are millions upon millions of tiny little self-replicating robots, all from one cup of coffee. Every single cell of you is being invaded. You're being embalmed alive. A human sculpture." The eyes were almost lifeless now. Packham stepped back, and flicked a switch on the wall. The rest of the studio lit up in a blaze of light, and half a dozen familiar statues became visible. He went back up to the youth, took out a silk handkerchief, and carefully wiped away the trail of spittle from the corner of his mouth.

"You should consider yourself lucky," he said. "Take a look at poor Venus over there. I have a feeling that she was still alive when I cut her arms off, you know." He paused. The eyes were completely dead. Packham leant forward and kissed the boy lightly on the lips.

"David, my David . . ." he whispered.

SIDELONG

It was a vicious and unprovoked sidelong attack – from someone claiming to be a knight as well. But we were just pawns to him.

CANINE MATHEMATICS

The dog stared at me with what seemed to be disgust.

"Look at the state of you," it said.

"I know," I replied, contrite. After seven or eight pints of lager, there's nothing much unusual about a talking dog.

I say seven or eight pints, but drinking is subject to some kind of pseudo-Heisenberg principle, where the ability to measure the quantity consumed is inversely proportional to that quantity. If I'd been remotely sober, I could have probably put together some kind of formal equation, but after the aforementioned seven-or-eight-plus-or-minus-delta pints, it was a hopeless task, and I gave up after a few desultory attempts. This was before I met the dog.

I was sitting on a park bench staring down at the pool of vomit between my feet. The shape of the pool was irregular, and I was considering the possibilities of complex integration around the curve of its perimeter when a further wave of reverse peristalsis forced its way out and distorted it.

The dog was still watching me, suspiciously.

"Do you realise what you're doing to the olfactory gradients around here?" it said, cocking its head on one side. "How am I going to find my way past here for the next few days when there's that whiff throwing me off course?"

"Sorry," I mumbled. The dog continued to stare at me. It was a golden retriever. I've had a few encounters with golden retrievers on my way home from drinking in my time, although that isn't say that I haven't met my fair share of spaniels, poodles and labradors. There's no real pattern to it, apart from the fact that they tend to talk to me in this tediously moralistic and higher-than-thou tone of voice. I am beginning to loathe dogs.

"How's the work going, anyway?" it said.

"It's fine. Or, at least, my funding's been renewed for next year, at least."

"Really?"

"Yup. Now, look, I hope you don't mind, but I'd rather you didn't keep talking to me like this. People may be watching."

"I could help you."

"I doubt it."

"You reckon? See that vomit of yours? Here's a rough equation for its perimeter." It scrawled a few vague lines on the pavement with its paw.

"Ah," I said.

"Well, what do you think?"

"It's just a load of scratches."

The dog rolled its eyes. "Well, you might think that, but I assure you that it's anything but." It called out to a passing mongrel, who came over and nodded furiously, before declaring, "A few inaccuracies in the higher level terms, but fundamentally sound." Then it trotted off into the night.

"You see?" said the retriever, making a few minor adjustments. "You're just not understanding the terminology."

"Can't you write a proper equation instead?"

"A proper equation? You're joking. You humans make things far too complicated. I wouldn't have the time or the patience. No, if you want to understand, you'll need to learn how to do canine maths."

"You're taking the piss, aren't you?" I said, exasperated.

"Certainly not. Are you?" it countered.

"I don't need to justify myself. My mathematics is absolute. That's why it's called Pure Mathematics. It does what it says on the tin."

"There are no absolutes," said the dog. "Whatever fundamental principles you derive, they'll simply reflect the way your brain is made. The same with ours, except that we learnt long ago to express our mathematics in a universal language."

"I don't believe this."

"I'll prove it," said the dog, waving a paw at a ginger tom who was up a nearby tree. The cat leapt down and came over warily, keeping its distance.

"What do you think?" said the retriever to the cat. It sat staring at the scratches on the pavement for a minute or two, deep in thought.

"Well," it said eventually, in a surprisingly deep voice, "it's fundamentally sound, but you need to use a more accurate multiple of ϖ." Then it turned and shot up the tree again.

"See?" said the dog.

In my office, I am staring at a sheet of paper covered in scratches. It still doesn't make any sense to me. I lied to the dog: my funding application is still awaiting approval. If I could just come up with some new insights into complex integration, I might just swing it. But I didn't get the dog's address, and in any case I have a horrible feeling that he may have been lying to me as well.

UPWARDLY MOBILE

Her origins were humble, but the clergy and gentry would all soon learn to respect her. One more square and she'd be a queen.

SOMEWHAT LESS
THAN THIRTY PIECES

"I have to say that I'm more than a little disappointed," announces Mr Fisher, testily.

Ooh, he won't like that. It's a triple whammy. Opening with dialogue, followed by the use of a redundant speech tag. And a bloody adverb. Mind you, I've never really got what it is that is so wrong with adverbs. Surely the big-deal writers use them all the time. How did they get away with something like "Truly, Madly, Deeply"?

Actually, how *did* they get away with something like "Truly, Madly, Deeply"?

Oh, let's try again.

Mr Fisher puts his jacket on the back of his chair and eyes us all with a certain amount of contempt.

"I have to say that I'm more than a little disappointed," he says. "I don't have to come here, you know; there are a thousand and one other things I'd rather be doing on a wet Tuesday evening in November. If you can't be bothered to do the work I set, it's not worth bothering to turn up to this class. As I've said many, many times before, you're not going to get anywhere at all without a proper level of commitment." He heaves a sigh and shrugs his shoulders in an unnecessarily theatrical manner. "But, as I say – it's up to you."

A classic passive-aggressive little tantrum from Mr Fisher, there, and I think I have caught it rather well, even if I say so myself. But he hasn't finished.

"So, then. Betrayal. Not a particularly difficult thing to write about, is it?" His eyes range over the room, as we mumble our negative responses. I am half expecting a panto-mimic "I didn't quite hear you, what did you say?" from him, but he's not in a mood for playing games.

"So why is it that out of all of you in this class," he says, "I have so far received just one single piece of work on the subject? Is it really that hard to come up with something? Consider this: man has been stabbing his fellow man in the back since the dawn of time. The act of betrayal is so deeply ingrained in Western culture, you could almost make a case for saying that the history of Western culture is the history of betrayal. After all, betrayal lies at the heart of the Christian *mythos*. Think about it. Who is the most famous betrayer of all time?"

Someone (not me) mutters "Judas". Mr Fisher smiles at last. He has got a response. Ditzy Jemima on the other side of the room is looking terribly pleased with herself. I'm guess-ing now that (1) she is the proud author of the only piece to have been submitted and that (2) she has written it about Judas. My reason for guess #1 is that she has been frantically shagging Mr Fisher for the last couple of months and will do almost anything to please him. My reason for guess #2 is that she is terminally shallow. Actually, that has a lot to do with guess #1 as well, now I come to think about it.

"So, then, consider Judas," says Mr Fisher. "Is it still pos-sible to write an original story about Mr Iscariot? Can any of you come up with an original angle?"

"Mrs Iscariot!" shouts one of the bikers at the back. They do a nice line in horror, combined with gratuitously graphic sex. There is, however, a surprising level of lyricism discern-ible in their work. If you look very, very hard.

Mr Fisher ignores him. Evidently the question was rhetorical. "Perhaps we could add another twist to the tale, so that Peter in fact betrays Judas by tricking him into betraying Jesus . . ."

Ditzy Jemima is smiling so much her head looks like it may well split in two along its equator.

" . . . and we could almost make a convincing case for that. Here's Peter, the pushy upstart who's after Big J's job – indeed, he will soon deny him three times – and there's poor old Judas, the patsy . . ."

Ditzy Jemima is almost bouncing up and down in her seat now. I shake my head sadly. This is not going to end well.

". . . but to propose such a jejune conceit would be to descend to the level of a particularly dense GCSE English class, I'm afraid."

Ditzy Jemima is staring at Mr Fisher in disbelief. He raises his eyebrows at her, shrugs, and – good Lord! – flashes a sneaky little grin over to where Quiet Barbara in the corner is sitting. Quiet Barbara is beaming all over her face. What are those two up to, then?

Suddenly, at nearly 800 words in, I am sensing a whole new layer to the story. I glance at the Goth chick at the desk next to mine, with a slight tilt of the head as if to say, "Did you see that?" She nods back in a dreamy Goth sort of way. I have no idea who she is, or what she writes about. She just drifts into the class, lurks in the shadows for a couple of hours and then drifts out again.[1]

"So, then," says Mr Fisher, as Ditzy Jemima runs crying out

---

1 Actually, this isn't strictly true. It turns out that her name is Krystal, and she is writing a long and complex novel about the love between vampires and zombies. In the pub afterwards, over a Guinness with a rum and black chaser, she tells me that the plot of her novel hinges on a doomed affair between a beautiful female vampire and a hunky macho zombie who can never touch for fear of destroying each other. Inevitably, in the grand finale of the book, they share a night of desperate, passionate sex, following which they die horribly in each others arms. Or something like that.

Whatever, I take this shared intimacy as the green light to make my move on Krystal, which – pleasingly – is not rebuffed, and we enjoy a similar night of passion ourselves, although with a less tragic outcome. Like all Goths I've known, she is a serious and considerate lover, with some interesting piercings to boot. She is, however, extremely pissed off to find out that she has ended up as a mere footnote to my story, and flatly refuses to see me again afterwards.

of the room, "in the absence of any other work to discuss, we shall spend the rest of the class writing the piece on betrayal that we failed to write in the previous week. Any questions? Good." Mr Fisher immediately goes over to Quiet Barbara's desk and begins an earnest, whispered conversation. All the time, she gazes up in awe at him, playing with her hair. Wonder if he's got his leg over yet? If not, it won't be long until he does.

After a while, he pats her gently on her shoulder and goes over to Mad Olive in the corner. Mad Olive is a poet. I don't think I need to say any more, do I? He briefly studies Mad Olive's work in progress with a sympathetic, yet baffled, eye, and moves off shaking his head from side to side. He pauses to have a quick word with the bikers, who are both scribbling away furiously and clearly not interested in discussing anything. Mr Fisher is slightly afraid of the bikers. I suspect he is afraid of all men. Within these four walls, as the sole published author, he is the alpha male, however weedy and hopeless he may otherwise be as a human being. However, you can tell that there is still bubbling under the surface a small but significant echo of the inadequacy he feels as soon as he steps outside the door.

He is standing behind me now.

"Ah," says Mr Fisher. "So we're off on another post-modern kick, are we?"

As he peers over my shoulder, trying to make out what I am writing, I manoeuvre myself so that he can read as little as possible of it. I want to finish this before he has a chance to criticise it. Eventually, he abandons the over-the-shoulder point of view and comes round in front of me, and is now attempting to read it upside down.

After ploughing through nearly 1200 words of it, his mind starts to drift off into a little world of its own, where he is cupping Quiet Barbara's firm breasts in his hands, as she moans to him: yes, yes, yes . . . but his reverie is rudely interrupted by the realisation of an egregious point-of-view switch. He tuts to himself before reading on.

"I take it that you've asked everyone in the room's permission if you can include them in your work." he says. "I wouldn't want you to be betraying any confidences." He looks around to emphasise the point. I wonder briefly if it's worth trying to highlight the fact that I have just uncovered another layer of betrayal, but it's pretty weak, to be honest.

Anyway, this is why I have changed his name to Mr Fisher. I was tempted for a few seconds to change it to something like Mr Weasel or Mr Gitface, but that would just be too easy. "Mr Fisher" is neutral. "Mr Fisher" carries no baggage. Mr Fisher is also still staring at my work.

"This really won't do. Having a writer as the main character is such a cliché. And what's with all the footnotes?[2] What is the bloody point of the piece, for God's sake?"

"I'm examining the concept of betrayal from a number of different angles," I say.

"To what end? What light are you hoping to bring to bear on the subject?" Mr Fisher is clearly not impressed.

"Maybe I'm trying to show that betrayal is indeed as ubiquitous as you suggested earlier," I say.

"Yes, but simply putting your argument into direct speech isn't going to turn it from a tiresome polemic into a piece of fiction, I'm afraid. And it rather turns any chance of 'Show' into 'Tell', doesn't it?"

Oh God, show and tell. That's all we need now. "I suppose it does," I say.

"I might even go so far as to say that it's a betrayal of all you stand for as a writer. Well, I would if I felt that you'd come up with anything worthwhile since you've been in this class."

This isn't entirely fair. A couple of weeks back, I came up with a rather clumsy metaphor for sexual inadequacy involv-

2 I assert that there is nothing wrong with a good footnote (ask Krystal). Consider the work of Flann O'Brien or – more recently – Susanna Clarke, for example. If the truth were to be told, I think it's more a case of Mr Fisher having trouble with the small print and being too vain to wear reading glasses. Actually, come to think of it, maybe it's not a good idea to mention footnotes to Krystal. She's still a bit sore about that.

ing a broken coffee machine that he quite liked. But he seems to have forgotten that little triumph. Then his face brightens slightly.

"But maybe . . . just maybe . . . it might be possible to rescue it. If you can come up with a really original framing device. Although God knows what you're going to have to come up with to save this one." He pauses. "I do like the opening, though," he says, before moving on to talk to the mystery Goth on my right.[3]

A framing device? What on earth does he mean by that? If it's what I think he means, we're not doing that until next month. Ah, it's hopeless. I might as well tear the whole thing up and start again. I'm not even happy with the title. Should it be "Somewhat Less than Thirty Pieces" or "Somewhat Fewer Than Thirty Pieces"? The answer is the former if I am referring to the amount of silver paid to Judas, but the latter if I am referring to the number of pieces on "Betrayal" written for my evening class. Sometimes I wonder if I am trying too hard to be clever.

The vision fades, and Judas looks up.

"I'm still not sure that I really understand what it means," he says.

"Me neither, me old china," says Jesus. "But what I think it's saying – apart from the obvious point that 2000 years from now, literature is going to be in severe danger of disappearing up its own fundament – is that betrayal is part of our genetic makeup. It's what we do."

"So?"

"Chances are, you're probably going to betray me at some point anyway. So, if I were you, I'd take the thirty pieces of silver on offer and go ahead. I won't mind. Really. It's kind of part of the plan."

"But . . . my Lord, I can't—"

"Oh, go on, you know you can. Look, if you feel bad about

3 Yes, I know she's called Krystal. But she's still not speaking to me. The bitch.

it afterwards, have a bit of chocolate to cheer you up. That's what I always say, isn't it? And thirty pieces'll get you a really nice Easter egg."

Well, Christ knows if that's the kind of thing Mr Fisher's looking for. Anyway, time's up, so it hardly matters. I hand the piece in to him and he acknowledges it with a grunt that tells me that he's not going to waste too much time on it. As I'm packing the rest of my stuff away, I happen to catch the eye of the Goth chick, and she gives me a translucent, Gothic smile. "Fancy a drink?" I say.

ACKNOWLEDGEMENTS

There are two possible approaches to be taken when writing the acknowledgements section of a book. First of all, there's the specific one, wherein the writer gives a vast list of friends, relations and minor acquaintances, always ending with the ubiquitous ananyonelsooknowsme.

The problem with this approach is that you always end up leaving someone important out, wiping out any kudos gained by mentioning the people you actually do remember to thank. I left at least one significant person out of the acknowledgements for *Mrs Darcy versus the Aliens* (and if you're thinking it was you, of course it was) and I've felt terrible ever since.

So I'm going to go for the safer general approach this time. Thanks as ever to my wonderful family. Thanks to all the various literary folk who have inspired, encouraged and challenged me over the last few years, starting with the wonderful Verulam Writers' Circle. Thanks also to the amazing people who run the online forums, small presses, spoken word events and competitions that are the lifeblood of every fledgling writer. And finally, thanks to Chris and Jen at Salt for being the best publishers ever.

All of the dashes and most of the dots have previously been either published or placed in competitions. Here's where:

DOTS

'Not So Much a Rough Guide' and all four parts of 'Love Story' were published by *PicFic*. 'The Drought' was published by *escarp*. 'Surveillance' was published by *Outshine*. 'Steaming' was published by *Thaumatrope*. 'Pulse' was a finalist and audience award winner in the 2010 NYC Midnight Tweet Me a Story contest. 'Fair Trade', Sidelong' and 'Upwardly Mobile' were all published by Seedpod Publishing. 'Internal Affairs' was published in *Flashshot*. 'Think Tank' was commended in the 2009 Leaf Nano-Fiction competition and was published in the subsequent anthology. 'After the Rapture' and 'Less Than Deadly' were both published by *Tweet the Meat*. 'Misunderstandings' was published by *Tuesday Shorts*. 'The Experiment' was a top-25 finalist in the 2011 NYC Midnight Tweet Me a Story contest. 'Perfect Moment' was published by *One Forty Fiction*. 'Big Teeth' and 'Proper Job' were both published in *VSS Anthology 01*; 'Proper Job' was also highly commended in the *txtlit* competition. 'Making Conversation' was published by *Trapezemag*. 'Bad Grammar' was a finalist and audience award winner in the 2011 NYC Midnight Tweet Me a Story contest. 'Under the Statue' was published by *Nanoism*. 'So What Are You Up To These Days?' and 'Tribute Act' were both published in *Six Sentences*. 'Opposites' was published by *Vestal Review*.

DASHES

'rZr and Napoleon' was shortlisted in the 2009 Fish Short Story Competition; it was also shortlisted in the 2010 Bristol Short Story Competition and published in the subsequent anthology. 'Convalescence' won 3rd prize in the 2007 University of Hertfordshire Writing Award and was published in the subsequent anthology, *Vision*. 'Mathematical Puzzles and Diversions' was read at Liars' League. 'The Amazing Arnolfini and His Wife' won 2nd prize in the 2008 City of Derby Short Story Competition and was also broadcast by the BBC as part of their *Opening Lines* season in 2010. 'Breathe In, Breathe Out' was published as part of the *Greyling Bay* project. 'Nature's Banquet' won 1st prize in Earlyworks' Press Old Magic in a New Age competition and was published in the subsequent anthology. 'Return to Cairo' won 3rd prize in the 2009 City of Derby Short Story Competition. 'The Problem with Pork' won a Supplementary Prize in the 2009 Bournemouth Short Story Competition and was published in the subsequent anthology; under its previous name 'Meat', it was also longlisted in the 2007 Fish Short Story Competition. 'Natural Selection' was published by *Short Story Radio*. 'Possible Side Effects' won 3rd prize in the 2009 Calderdale Short Story Competition. 'Mr Nathwani's Haiku' won 3rd place in the 2008 Winchester Writers' Conference Shorter Short Story Competition. 'Anniversary Feast' was published in *Fifty-Two Stitches*. 'How I Became a New Man and What Good It Did Me' was shortlisted in the Spring 2010 JBWB Competition. 'The Guitarist's Inheritance' was published by *apt*. 'Fishermen's Tales' won 2nd prize in the 2008 Milton Keynes Speakeasy Competition; under its previous name 'Catch of the Day', it was also highly commended in a JBWB Short Story Competition. 'Hidden Shallows' and 'Mirror, Mirror' were both published by *Every Day Fiction*. 'Advice re Elephants' was shortlisted in the 2010 Seán Ó Faoláin competition, and was also subsequently published in *Metazen*. 'The Birdman of Farringdon Road' and 'Piss and Patchouli' were both published by *Litro*; 'Piss and Patchouli' was also longlisted in a *Cadenza* competition. 'A Plague of Yellow Plastic Ducks' was published by *Abacot Journal*. 'The Magnolia Bedroom' was shortlisted in the Global Short Story Competition and was also published in the 2009 Whittaker Prize anthology. 'The Last Words of Emanuel Prettyjohn' was shortlisted in the 2009 Southport Writers' Circle Competition. 'Farewell Symphony' was read at Tales of the Decongested and was also published in the 2009 Whittaker Prize anthology. 'At Nana's' won 2nd prize in the 2007 Bournemouth Literary Festival Erotic Writing Competition. 'After Michelangelo' was published by *Necrotic Tissue*; a different version was also performed on several occasions as a staged reading by Obstacle Productions. 'Canine Mathematics' was published by *Smokebox* and also read at SPARKS. 'Somewhat Less Than Thirty Pieces' was longlisted in a *Cadenza* competition and subsequently published by *TheRightEyedDeer*, where it was nominated for a Best of the Net award. 'Convalescence', 'The Amazing Arnolfini and His Wife' and 'The Birdman of Farringdon Road' are also all published as mobile phone stories by Ether Books.